STOLEN BLESSINGS

Lawrence Sanders

Stolen Blessings

BERKLEY BOOKS, NEW YORK

STOLEN BLESSINGS

A Berkley Book/published by arrangement with
the author

Quality Printing and Binding by:
Orange Graphics
P.O. Box 791
Orange, VA 22960 U.S.A.

STOLEN BLESSINGS

Beverly Hills, CA

The Most Beautiful Woman in the World, known to Hollywood film producers as Attila the Huness, comes striding into the headquarters of Marilyn Taylor Enterprises, Inc., on El Camino Drive. Fear and trepidation precede her; pandemonium follows.

She tells the trembling receptionist never, but *never,* to wear that blouse again. "Bile green makes my teeth ache."

She tells Murray, the nerdish gofer, to bring her a spicy Bloody Maria (made with tequila). "I want a stalk of celery *and* a wedge of lime."

She tells her comptroller, Benjamin Geltman, to double-check the inventory figures of the Marilyn Taylor Lingerie, Inc., boutique in Spokane. "If they're for real, have the manager arrested."

She tells her attorney, A. Stewart Roche, that the proposed contract with Magnum Pathway Films for *Joan of Arkansas* is unacceptable. "I want half of the eight mil up front."

She tells Loretta Donovan, her black beautician, that she wants silver toenails. "Something with a high gloss."

She tells her flack, Gary Flomm, to have the film critic of *Cinema Today* fired because of his review of her performance in a remake of *Rebecca of Sunnybrook Farm.* When Flomm, giggling maniacally, suggests that might be difficult, Marilyn says wrathfully, "Then have his kneecaps smashed. Let the sonofabitch get around on a skateboard."

She tells Shari, the Italian designer for Marilyn Taylor Fashions, Inc., to lower the neckline of the new gold lamé evening gown. "T and A, sweetie; that's what we're selling—tits and ass."

She tells her secretary, Harriet Boltz, to make certain the corporate jet is fueled and ready to go. "And be sure there's plenty of bubbly aboard."

She tells Sidney, her perfumed hairdresser, that he'll travel to New York with her. "Bring the black wig and fall. You might pack the punk job, too —just for laughs."

She tells her wetback bodyguard, Tony Perez, that he'll carry her jewel case. "Lose that, and you'll lose *your* jewels."

Then they crowd into her private office, a spacious chamber decorated with photographs of producers, directors, leading men, and film critics, all framed in white enameled toilet seats.

She strips down to bra and panties, sits in the black leather swivel chair

behind her teak desk, and is draped with a flowered sheet from Marilyn
Taylor Linens, Inc. She sips her Bloody Maria while her strawberry blond
curls are artfully teased and her toenails are silvered with High Moon, a
polish from Marilyn Taylor Cosmetics, Inc. She replies to a dozen questions from her staff, giving prompt, definite, and frequently profane answers.

She also takes a dozen phone calls: stockbroker, investment adviser,
shrink, gynecologist, reporters. Requests for contributions, interviews, autographed photos. Offers of movie roles. Pleas for loans. And invitations to
luncheons, dinners, premieres, orgies, and charity balls. She gives the same
answer to all: she's on her way to New York. Call her when she returns in,
oh, maybe three or four weeks.

The most persistent caller is Sam Davidson, a scoundrel who produced
her first movie and has never let her forget it. It was called *Private Parts,*
and made a mint for Davidson. But he never hit again, lost all his money
on dry oil wells, and the talk is that he's now producing X-rated videos,
many of them featuring a hyperkinetic orangutan. He has a wild dream of
producing *Private Parts, II,* starring Marilyn Taylor.

He becomes so importunate that in a few thousand well-chosen words—
her awed staff listening—she tells him exactly what she thinks of him,
starting with "Listen, you asshole . . ." In the low, throaty voice that has
thrilled millions, she comments on his appearance, his talent, his canine
ancestry, his business ethics, and his sexual habits. Finally, just before she
slams down the phone, she tells him that if he continues his harassment,
she'll send a couple of heavies to excise his testicles without the benefit of
an anesthetic.

Then, Bloody Maria finished, curls teased, toenails painted, Marilyn
chases everyone out of the office except Harriet Boltz, a tough little broad
who wears tweed suits and uses a monocle to read the fine print.

"Well, kiddo," says The Most Beautiful Woman in the World, "off we go
to the Big McIntosh to seek fame and fortune."

"Those you got," her secretary says. "Look, Marilyn, are you sure you
want to go through with this?"

"Sure, I'm sure. It's just a simple operation—no worse than a D and C."

"That's not what I mean. I'm talking about the other."

"Oh, hell, Harry, it's just the smart thing to do. I've had more abortions
than you've had permanents, and I'm tired of it. Might as well get it over
with once and for all."

"You may regret it," Harriet says darkly. "Someday."

"Not me. I like my life just the way it is."

"Bullshit," her secretary says.

Early that evening, about 5:30 P.M., Carl Seaman, the chauffeur, pulls up in the gray stretch Mercedes limousine. He is followed by a rented Lincoln Towncar. Marilyn Taylor and her staff get their luggage loaded, then pile into the two cars.

Not making the trip to New York are attorney A. Stewart Roche and comptroller Benjamin Geltman. They wave goodbye on the sidewalk, then return to Roche's office. He breaks out a bottle of Chivas Regal and pours each of the fatsoes a shot in a paper cup.

"Take away her face and her figure," he says, "and what have you got?"

"A skeleton who breaks balls," Geltman says.

Brooklyn, NY

Turk's Bar is a real bucket of blood, grungy even by Atlantic Avenue standards. Ask for a *very* dry martini, up with twist, and you'll be lucky to get out of the joint alive. It's wiser to order a straight shot, and when the mastodonic bartender demands, "What'll youse have for a wash?", tell him meekly that a short beer will do you fine. You won't be accepted, but you'll be tolerated.

In the back room, the floor littered with sawdust, peanut shells, and antique cigar butts, three men sit at a ramshackle table nursing their boilermakers. Two are dressed with all the panache of Dutch Schultz. The third wears the soiled whites of a medical orderly or laboratory technician.

The man in white is Nicholas Kazanian, employed by a Manhattan fertility clinic. The other two, Solomon Pincus and Joseph ("Dumbo") Abruzzi, work as mail sorters at the Brooklyn post office. All three are obsessive and remarkably inept horseplayers to whom the daily and dismal report on their selections, "Out of the money," has come to be the knell of doom.

Now, heads together, they discuss Kazanian's scheme to rescue them all from chronic penury.

"First of all," Nick says, "you've got to admit she's got all the money in the world. Am I right?"

"Plus, she's a looker," Solly says, scrubbing his bald dome. "That face! That chassis! Also, she can act."

"Yeah, well," Dumbo says, "so life is unfair. Tell me something I don't know."

"The important thing is that she's got the lettuce," Nick goes on. "And the way I figure it, she'll pay off quietly. No cops or anything like that. I mean a woman in her position just won't want any publicity. It's too personal—know what I mean?"

"Listen," Abruzzi says, blinking behind thick glasses, "run through it again—okay?"

Kazanian sighs. "All right, one more time. It's really very simple. Here's how it works: Every month a woman produces an egg."

"That's the part I don't get," Dumbo says. "Chickens lay eggs, not bimbos. They have babies."

"And where the hell do you think babies come from?" Solly asks.

"Maybe the stork brings bring them? The baby starts with the egg. Am I right, Nick?"

"Right. A woman produces an egg. It's not like a chicken egg with a shell. It's a little bitty thing. If there was one on this table right now, you'd never even see it. So then the woman gets humped. The guy's jism has got these zillions of sperm in it. They look like weeny tadpoles. If just one of those tadpoles hits the woman's egg—bingo!—you've got a baby. Now the point is that a lot of women can't produce an egg. Maybe they're sick or their plumbing is rusty. But they want to have a baby. So what do they do? They borrow an egg from a girlfriend. Well, maybe not *borrow* because that egg is never going to be paid back. But a girlfriend gives them an egg, or maybe they buy one from a professional."

"Holy cow!" Solly says. "You mean women make a living selling their eggs?"

"Nah. Not yet they don't. But they can pick up a nice piece of change, like maybe five C's, by selling their eggs to a woman who wants to have a baby. Now what they do is have this woman's husband jack off in a little jar. They combine the guy's sperm with the donated egg, and after the baby gets started—it's smaller than a pinhead—they shove it up the old ox road, and the woman gets pregnant. How do you like that?"

Dumbo shakes his head. "I still don't understand it. I know who the father is—he's the guy in the jar—but who's the mother?"

"Well, actually the baby will have two mothers: the one who donated the egg and the one who has the kid. But you don't have to worry about that. We're going to score with the eggs. Kidnap them and hold them for ransom. The most famous eggs in the world! I've got it all worked out, and we can't miss. We'll make a mint!"

"Wait a minute," Solly says slowly. "Something here don't wash. You say a woman produces an egg a month?"

"Usually. Sometimes more than one. They shoot her full of hormones, and she can produce a dozen."

"So what's the point of kidnapping a woman's eggs? She's not going to pay to get them back if she'll have a new batch next month."

Nicholas Kazanian leans forward with a secret smile. "That's the beauty part," he says softly.

Manhattan, NY

The headquarters of Marilyn Taylor Merchandise, Inc. (dolls, photos, posters, video cassettes, etc.), are located in a six-story town house on East 63rd Street. The first three floors are offices. The remainder of the handsome limestone building is occupied by The Most Beautiful Woman in the World and her personal staff when they are in New York.

This lavish pied-à-terre has its own staff: houseman, maid, housekeeper, chef. There are several bedrooms and bathrooms, living room, dining room, a small screening room, and a smaller gym.

After dinner on her second night in Manhattan, Marilyn and her two guests move into the living room. Eve and Eric Bannon are a married couple, about the same age as their hostess. They have driven into the city from their home in Scarsdale, where Eve is a housewife and Eric a junior partner with Rimbaugh, Fliese, Gobal, Handringham, Mimsett, Norrington & Tubbs. (Their receptionist, understandably, answers the phone by drawling, "Law office.")

"I went to see Doc Primster this afternoon," Marilyn tells the others after they have been served espresso and Frangelico, and the houseman has left the room. "He checked me out, and the hormones are working. He figures what he calls 'optimum ovulation' in another three or four days. So the two of you better stand by. Primster doesn't want to waste any time."

"Marilyn, we can't thank you enough," Eric says, gripping his wife's hand. "You're really giving us the gift of life."

She looks at them with some amusement. They are both blond, glowing, and sappy with love. "Cut the hearts-and-flowers shit," she says to Eric. "I'm not doing it *all*, you know. You're the guy who's going to have to whack off. By the way, Primster showed me the room where you'll do your dirty deed. It's called the Masturbatorium—can you believe it? Soft lights, low music, centerfolds taped to the walls. All the comforts of home."

"It's my fault," Eve wails. "If my stupid tubes weren't blocked, we wouldn't have to go through all this. But I can't tell you how happy and excited I am about getting your egg. I want a baby girl, and I want her to be just as beautiful as you are."

"And if it's a boy," her husband says, "I hope he inherits your talent and ambition."

"Yeah?" the star says, looking at the two closely. "No regrets now or in the future that your kid will be half mine?"

"Are you joking?" Eve says hotly. "We'll be *proud*. Won't we, honey?"

"Absolutely," Eric says. "I just wish we could tell the world what a great thing you're doing for us."

"Not for you, buster," Marilyn says roughly. "I'm doing it for Eve. Your wife and I went through the audition wars together when we were penniless ninnies trying to get a break on Broadway. Eve, you're the one who slung hash to keep us going. I've never forgotten that. I owe you one, kiddo; I'm just paying my dues. As for telling people—no way! I know, you know, my secretary knows, and the people at the clinic. But no one else is to be told, and I mean *no* one! I'm not doing this for the publicity. I'll get my reward when your little bit of heaven pees in my arms. But what if it's twins—ever think of that? With all the fertility drugs we've been taking, it could be twins or even triplets."

"Marvelous!" Eve cries. "The more the merrier. I never made it in the theater, but this is a part I know I can play: the great earth mother."

They talk for another hour about the planned laparoscopies, the *in vitro* fertilization of Marilyn's egg by Eric's sperm, and the implanting of the resulting zygote in Eve's uterus. Then the Bannons rise and both embrace Marilyn Taylor, snuffling with joy and gratitude.

"I hope," she says, pushing them away, "I hope the next time I see you two monsters you'll be well on your way to being momma and papa."

After they leave, she is unaccountably depressed, and yells upstairs for Harriet. The secretary comes into the room carrying a bottle of Rémy Martin.

"After an evening with the Bobbsey Twins," she says, "I figured you could use a shot."

"Right on," Marilyn says. "I love them both, but they're always so goddamned *up*, it wears on the nerves."

Harriet pours them snifters of cognac. "Did you tell them you're going to be sterilized at the same time?"

"Hell, no! They have no need to know."

"Why *are* you doing it?"

"Who wants a smelly brat around the house? Eve does, but not me."

"Uh-huh," Harriet says, staring at her. "You know what I think it is? I think you're frightened. I think the idea of getting pregnant and popping a kid scares the bejesus out of you. It's not only the mess and pain, but you're afraid having a baby will ruin your figure—and there goes your career. It's an ego thing with you."

"Thank you, Dr. Freud," Marilyn says. "Now shut your yap and pour me another jolt."

They kick off their shoes, put their feet up on the cocktail table, and drink in silence awhile.

"Was she a good actress?" Harriet asks finally.

"Eve? Better than I am. But she never had the drive. She was never willing to put out for a producer."

"Well, those days are over."

"That's right," says Marilyn Taylor, smiling coldly. "Now it's vicey versy."

Staten Island, NY

Ronald Yates, a thirty-four-year-old teenager with all the hopeless dreams and melodramatic fears of the breed, leaves his job as assistant chef de cuisine of the Yum-Yum Burger Shoppe in West New Brighton and drives home in his old Volkswagen Beetle. It might have been a collector's item if it wasn't rusted out, the trunk tied shut with a piece of rope, a tattered tape ineffectively closing a leak in the roof, and a big Yum-Yum decal pasted on the rear window.

On the seat beside him is a greasy bag containing his mother's dinner: three Giant Cheez-Burgers, two large portions of Zippy Fries, two bottles of black cherry cola, and a Yum-Yum Mom's Apple Pie. The pie is four days old but so chockablock with chemical preservatives that it can last a month before turning an iridescent green.

The residence of Ronnie and his mother, Mrs. Gertrude Yates, is more bungalow than house. But there is a one-car garage, a weed-throttled lawn, one feeble ailanthus tree, and a cracked concrete birdbath usually filled by local roisterers with empty beer cans and used condoms.

Gertrude Yates lives her life on the first floor since she has become so shockingly obese that she requires aid to rise from her reinforced chair. She sleeps in what was originally a small dining room, being incapable of climbing the stairs to the bedroom she once occupied with her husband, Horace Yates, who decamped years ago.

Ronnie now has the second floor to himself. It would be a secluded private apartment if it wasn't for the constant blare of his mother's 41-inch television set downstairs. He sleeps in the master bedroom. The second bedroom—the door always kept locked—has been converted into a shrine.

The walls are covered with posters and photographs of Marilyn Taylor. The posters show her in bikini, negligee, babydoll pajamas, and slinky evening gown. There are advertisements of her films and of her increasingly rare appearances on the Broadway stage. The photos are glossies (two of them autographed "To Ronnie, my favorite fan"), plus magazine covers, newspaper clippings, and one portrait, hand-colored and framed in imitation wood, sold by Marilyn Taylor Merchandise, Inc.

There are bound copies of the *Marilyn Taylor Fanette,* a quarterly periodical published by the International Marilyn Taylor Fan Club (almost wholly financed by Marilyn Taylor Enterprises, Inc.). Beneath the magazine's logo is a quotation from a profile of Marilyn that appeared in *Time:* "The most universally beloved film star since Mickey Mouse."

Ronnie has a 25-inch TV set in his shrine, a VCR, and a shelf of all of Marilyn's movies available on video cassette. And there is a choice collection of personal memorabilia: a rose, a cigarette butt, and a pair of panties. She flung the rose to admirers during a personal appearance at a fundraiser. Ronnie was lucky enough to catch the tossed flower, and although he was immediately offered ten dollars for it by other fans, its faded petals are now lovingly pressed between two sheets of clear plastic.

He also has a cigarette butt she discarded, the tip still incarnadined with her lipstick. And best of all, a pair of brief nylon panties sold by Marilyn Taylor Lingerie, Inc., with the name *Marilyn* embroidered across the seat in what is alleged to be her very own script.

But on this particular evening, Ronald Yates has no time to enjoy his treasures. That afternoon, in Suzy's column in the New York *Post,* he read that Marilyn Taylor and her entourage had arrived in Manhattan and taken up residence at her "posh digs" on East 63rd Street.

Ronnie showers hurriedly, washing his lank straw hair to rid it of fumes from the grill at the Yum-Yum Burger Shoppe. Then he dresses in a clean T-shirt, freshly laundered jeans, and a black leather jacket exactly like the one worn by Marilyn's leading man in the hit musical *The Merchant of Venus.*

"Be back later!" Ronnie yells at his mother as he departs. But she pays no attention, sitting there with her orange hair in pink plastic curlers, eyes fixed on the giant television screen. It's a new game show, "Get Rich or Die."

He drives the VW toward the Staten Island ferry terminal, energized by the trip to Manhattan. He expects to find other fans clustered outside her home on East 63rd, and maybe a few paparazzi. Yates knows them all; they are coreligionists. There will be excited talk about why Marilyn has come to New York, what her next film will be, and the male celebrities with whom she has been romantically linked in the gossip columns.

And maybe, just maybe, during the evening she will come to a front window, pull the curtain aside, smile, and wave down to the faithful. That brief glimpse of the goddess in the flesh is all Ronnie Yates desires. It will be reward enough for his long trip.

But even if the lights of the town house are extinguished, and she makes no personal appearance, still he will stand there, looking upward, yearning, yearning, content that he is close to her and willing to forget his job and go hungry and sleepless to prove his eternal devotion.

Manhattan, NY

Dr. Reginald Primster has a smile that's all teeth. (Marilyn to Harriet Boltz: "He looks like a constipated beaver.") But his eyes remain cold and wary, almost bleak. Perhaps he remembers when his fertility institute was an abortion clinic, and people left bombs on his doorstep.

"And did we notice any side effects from the drugs?" the doctor asks.

"Nope," Marilyn Taylor says blithely. "Everything normal."

"Glad to hear it. Sometimes those hormones result in hyperstimulation."

"With me, it'd be hard to tell."

Again, that chilly smile. "As we mentioned on your last visit, we believe you are approaching a time of optimum ovulation. We cannot be precise about these matters—the entire field is more art than science—but we expect your tests today will indicate that your egg or eggs will reach the proper stage of maturation on Saturday. We would like you here at nine o'clock in the morning, and if final tests confirm, we will retrieve the eggs and do the tubal ligation. Will that be satisfactory?"

"Sure."

"We have prepared the legal releases for your signature, and we suggest you read them carefully before signing."

"Oh, I'll sign," Marilyn says. "But before I do, I just want to be sure the incision won't spoil my bikini line."

"It will be a very small incision," the doctor assures her. "Perhaps a half inch. It should heal quickly without leaving a visible scar. And the moment the eggs are removed we will proceed with the sterilization process you have requested."

"Yeah, let's talk about that for a while. That's done while my belly is still open?"

"That's correct. We'll continue to use the laparoscope in addition to monitoring you with ultrasound. It will give us a picture of the oviducts or fallopian tubes." He points to a chart on the wall. "Ordinarily each tube is three to five inches long, with the lower ends opening into the uterus, or womb. You'll notice the upper ends are not connected to the ovaries. But they have flared openings that hold out a tiny fringe called fimbria. The fimbria are what ordinarily pluck the ripened egg from the ovaries. The egg would then enter the oviduct. Since the egg cannot move by itself, it is carried down the tube by interior hairlike projections that wave back and forth and move the egg along toward the uterus, a process that usually takes from three to six days. That is the time and the oviduct is the place where conception takes place, providing of course that fertile sperm are present and the egg is successfully impregnated. The fertilized egg then continues its trip to the uterus, where it embeds itself in the interior wall, and pregnancy proceeds."

"I'm beginning to get the picture," Marilyn says. "Eve Bannon can't get pregnant because her tubes are blocked—right?"

"Correct. We attempted macrosurgery, but it was unsuccessful. We then suggested a second procedure using microsurgical techniques, but Mrs. Bannon opted for embryo transfer: ET. In the movie, of course, it meant extraterrestrial. That's rather amusing, don't you think?"

"Oh, yeah," Marilyn says. "A howl. So to sterilize me, you're going to close my tubes. Am I right?"

"Before we discuss sterilization procedures, I must ask you again if you have considered your decision carefully. Most women requesting tubal ligation already have children. But you are a young woman, Miss Taylor. It may well be that in a few years you will deeply regret having had yourself sterilized. You do have other options, you know."

"You mean like condoms and abortions? No, I want to go ahead with the tubal ligation. After all, it is reversible, isn't it?"

Dr. Primster sighs. "When a woman asks about reversing the procedure, we are almost certain she is not sure that she is doing the right thing. To answer your question, we must tell you that *sometimes* tubal ligation can be reversed, but it is always a difficult procedure and the results cannot be guaranteed."

"Look," says Marilyn, "I'm not going to have second thoughts. Just tell me how long I'm going to be laid up this weekend."

"Not long at all. After a few hours in the recovery room, you should be able to return home. If we do these procedures on Saturday, we recommend you rest in bed on Sunday but unless there are unforeseen complications, you should be able to do anything you want on Monday."

"Then let's get on with it," Marilyn says determinedly. "Give me your goddamned papers, and I'll sign them."

Dr. Primster whisks documents from a desk drawer and hands them to The Most Beautiful Woman in the World, along with a ballpoint pen. Marilyn scrawls her signature swiftly without reading the releases.

"When are you going to put the fertilized eggs into Eve?" she asks.

"As soon as possible. If we retrieve sufficient mature eggs on Saturday, they'll be frozen until next week. Then the husband will provide sperm.

After fertilization, we usually wait for a four-cell embryo before implantation."

"You mean my eggs will be frozen for days? Poor little things."

The doctor stares at her a moment. "As recently as a year ago, we would have commenced the fertilization procedure immediately after culturing the eggs. However, everyone in the field recognized the importance of improving the technology of freezing and thawing eggs, and the technology *has* been refined so that the pregnancy rate is comparable to that of eggs that have not been frozen. It is a great advancement and, we must admit, a great relief."

"A relief?" Marilyn asks. "How so?"

Dr. Primster fidgets with papers on his desk, looking acutely uncomfortable. "There are two problems with storing frozen embryos. First of all, who actually owns the embryo: the woman who donated the egg or the man who provided the sperm? They may be strangers to each other, and a disagreement over which donor actually holds title to the frozen embryo could very likely end up in court."

"More work for lawyers," Marilyn says. "What's the other problem?"

"When more embryos are produced than are actually needed for implantation, the excess are either frozen for possible future transfer or destroyed. Some have claimed that destroying an embryo—even if it is judged unsuitable for implantation—is tantamount to abortion. We try to fertilize only as many eggs as are needed for implantation, usually three or four. Now, with our new technology, the excess eggs can be frozen in liquid nitrogen if the donor wishes to preserve them for possible future use. Unlike the issue of embryos, if the frozen eggs are eventually destroyed, there can be no possible ethical objections."

"Yeah," Marilyn says thoughtfully, "I can see where that makes things easier."

"Well now," the doctor says briskly, "enough lecturing; I think we better get on with your tests." He presses a button on his intercom, and a moment later a tall, saturnine gink dressed in hospital whites comes into the office.

"Nick, we'll be doing ultrasound in about twenty minutes," Primster tells him.

"Yes, doctor," says Nicholas Kazanian.

Hollywood, CA

It's been a bad day for Sam Davidson.

The bentnoses to whom he supplies X-rated video cassettes send around two Godzillas to remind him that he's falling behind schedule, both in production of tapes and paying the vigorish on his horrendous debt.

Then the female star of his current script, *Jungle Belles*, turns up coked to the gills, hardly able to stand up, let alone express orgiastic joy at being humped by an orangutan.

And that farshtunken animal! Its trainer, a real bubblehead, injects too much tranquilizer, and the fucking monkey won't do anything but grin and eat bananas.

Finally Sam gives up. He turns off the lights, sends everyone home, and retires to his ratty office. His wife is seated at the splintered desk, playing one of her interminable games of solitaire. Sam takes a warm wine cooler from the kaput fridge and flops into an armchair, the one with springs poking up through cracked vinyl.

He uncaps his cooler and takes a swig, then shudders with distaste. "I can remember," he says, "when all I used to drink was chilled Dom Perignon mixed with freshly squeezed orange juice."

His wife looks up from her cards. "A tough morning, Sam?"

"They're all tough. I'd slit my wrists if I could afford a new razor blade."

"What are we going to do—starve?"

"We haven't hocked your wedding ring yet, have we?"

"And we're not going to," she says, going back to her game. "Just forget about it. What did those two shtarkers want, anyway?"

"You know what they wanted: tapes and money. Or my ass."

"You don't think they'll try any rough stuff, do you?"

"Nah. Unless you consider a kick in the nuts as rough stuff. Syl, baby, into each life some rain must fall—but who figures on an effing cloudburst? I've got to try Marilyn Taylor again. It's my only hope."

"After the way she talked to you? That's not a hope, that's a delusion."

"All I want her to do is read the script for *Private Parts: Two*. Denny O'Keefe and I have been working on it for five years, and it's ready to go. It's got the juiciest scenes she'll ever play. Bang-bang action, great dialogue, a love story that'll tear your guts out; it's got everything. I could bring that sucker in for five mil. My God, with her loot, she could bankroll it herself. But the bitch won't even give me the time of day. And after all I did for her."

"What did you do for her? You paid her bupkes to show her tits."

"It made her a star, didn't it?"

"And it made you a millionaire—until you lost it all. My husband, the oil baron."

"Lay off, will you. It was just bad luck, that's all. But the one sure thing about luck is that sooner or later it's got to change."

"With you, it's only later."

"I tell you if I could get her to read the script, she'd go for it. She may be a bitch, but she's not a dumb bitch; she knows a good property when she sees one. I'm going to try her again."

"You can't. She's gone to New York. It was in the *Reporter.*"

"So? Planes leave for New York every hour. I'll fly east and get her to read the script even if I have to hold a gun on her while she does it."

"You hocked your gun—remember? And how are you going to buy a plane ticket? All your plastic has been canceled."

"Your wedding ring," he says.

"Oh Jesus!" his wife wails despairingly.

He departs that evening, carrying the script in a brown paper bag along with a salami on rye.

Brooklyn, NY

They're in the back room at Turk's, and Kazanian is treating his cohorts to a Friday night feast of corned beef and cabbage. The surly waiter drops the plates on the table like a jailer feeding a trio of felons.

"It's all set," Nick says, staring at Abruzzi and wondering how a guy can chew gum and eat cabbage at the same time. "She's going under the knife tomorrow morning. If everything is okay, she'll be out of there by late afternoon. Her eggs will be put in liquid nitrogen in what they call a Dewar flask. The kind we use are plastic and have a handle like a pail."

"Heavy?" Solly Pincus asks.

"Nah. It's like a big thermos jug. The nitrogen is to freeze the eggs. Keep them from spoiling. That stuff is *cold*. About minus 190 degrees centigrade. Don't try dipping your dork in it or you'll have a permanent hard-on."

They finish their meal swiftly and in silence. Then Nick calls for another round of boilermakers. They wait for their drinks before getting down to business again.

"So tomorrow," Kazanian goes on, "I'll say I'm going to work late, get caught up on my reports. It's Saturday; everyone else will take off early. I'll be the only one there at ten o'clock, and I'll unlock the door and let you guys in."

"Don't that finger you?" Pincus says. "The cops will figure it's an inside job."

"If she calls the cops—which I doubt. But if she does, I'll say someone banged on the door and said it was a medical emergency, so I opened up. Listen, it's happened twice before. Once it was a guy who had just got mugged and was all bloody. The other time it was a woman going into labor, and she couldn't get a cab to her hospital. Y'see, Primster has his shingle outside, and sick people who don't know what kind of a joint it is are always wanting to see the doc."

"Okay," Abruzzi says, "now we're inside. Then what happens?"

"I show you which flask has her eggs, and you glom onto it. But before you leave, you tie me up like you jumped me. There's plenty of adhesive tape around, so you can use that. Do a good job because when the watchman comes on at midnight, he's going to find me, and I want him to think I didn't have a chance. You can even put a hunk of tape across my mouth because you don't want me to yell—right? But don't cover my nose because I gotta breathe, don't I?"

"So now we got her eggs in the thermos," Pincus says. "What do we do then?"

"You go back to your car, lock the flask in the trunk, and go home like nothing happened."

"Hey, wait a minute," Abruzzi says, lighting up one of his black stogies. "I don't like the idea of that thing being in *my* car. What if I get rear-ended or something, and the cops find it."

"It's only for a day," Kazanian argues. "On Monday morning my brother is shipping out on a freighter. He always leaves me the key to his apartment while he's gone. It's on West 54th Street near Eighth Avenue. I look in occasionally while he's away to make sure no one has trashed the place. That's where we're going to keep the flask until we collect. So you only keep it in the trunk of your car until Monday. Just make sure it's propped upright and can't spill. I'll get it from you on Monday morning. Okay?"

"I'm working Monday morning," Dumbo says.

"So I'll get it when you quit work," Nick says, sighing. "Don't make a federal case out of this. It's a very simple plan and it'll go like silk; you'll see."

"When do you think we'll collect?" Pincus asks.

"A week," Kazanian says, shrugging. "Maybe two at the most. I'm not going to send her any letters. I'll handle it all from pay phones, keeping the calls short so they can't be traced."

"How much you gonna ask?" Abruzzi wants to know.

Nick stares at him. "A mil. A cool million."

Suddenly all of them, including Nick, are awed and thoughtful. Kazanian cheats regularly on his taxes. Pincus cheats regularly on his wife. And, whenever possible, Abruzzi leaps over subway turnstiles. But they are not *crooked* crooks.

Now, faced with the realization that they are involved in a million-dollar caper, fear begins to dull their hopes of replenishing their fortunes with an infusion of easy but undeniably illicit cash.

"A million?" Sol says, his voice croaky. "You think she'll spring for it?"

"Maybe we shouldn't be greedy," Dumbo says. "A hundred grand might go better."

"She'll cough up a million," Nick says, trying to sound assured. "That kind of gelt means nothing to her. The woman is a tycooness, with all those businesses she's got going for her. Also, she's promised her eggs to her best friend, and she won't want to renege on the deal. And remember, after tomorrow her egg-laying days are over. So what we'll have in that flask will be very valuable to her, and she'll pay anything to get it back. This is our chance to score and score big. Believe me, I know what I'm doing."

His henchmen remain silent, and Kazanian signals the waiter for another round of boilermakers.

Manhattan, NY

Eve Bannon and Harriet Boltz insist on accompanying her on that fateful day. The three women leave the East 63rd Street town house at 8:30 A.M. on Saturday. The star is wearing a silk trench coat and her trademark black trilby, the brim cocked down over one eye.

Before they can clamber into the stretch Cadillac limousine waiting at the curb, Marilyn is surrounded by a gaggle of fans, all thrusting pens and scraps of paper at her, clamoring for her autograph. She signs a half dozen, including one on the back of a T-shirt, then joins Eve and Harriet in the limousine.

Ronald Yates has been staring adoringly at his goddess from the fringes of the crowd. Seeing Marilyn get into the Cadillac, he dashes wildly for his battered Volkswagen, doubled-parked across the street. When the limousine pulls slowly away, Ronnie follows in the Beetle, determined to spend the day trailing the woman who, he has solemnly vowed, "Means more to me than life itself."

The Cadillac doesn't travel far; Dr. Primster's fertility institute is on East 70th Street. The limousine halts briefly; the three women alight and enter the clinic. Yates finds a parking slot near First Avenue and walks back to take up his vigil.

Inside, Eve and Harriet settle down in the waiting room with year-old copies of the *National Geographic* and *Quarter Horse Gazette.* Marilyn is ushered upstairs for a final series of tests and prepping for the surgical procedures.

Shortly after 11:00 A.M., she disrobes, climbs onto a padded gurney, and is covered with a sheet by the attending aide. She is wheeled into the operating room where two nurses, two assisting surgeons, and an anesthetist are already scrubbed, gowned, and masked. Marilyn is lifted onto the operating table and a general anesthetic is administered. It takes effect within minutes, and while awaiting the arrival of the chief surgeon, the operating room team cop a look under the sheet and are struck dumb by that tanned perfection.

During the next hour, Dr. Reginald Primster, peering through his laparoscope, succeeds in retrieving nine mature eggs. They are rushed to an adjacent laboratory for preliminary culturing and freezing. Meanwhile the surgeon proceeds with the tubal ligation. The two operations are completed in slightly less than two hours. By 2:00 P.M., Marilyn Taylor has been wheeled into the recovery room.

When she regains consciousness, Eve Bannon and Harriet Boltz are standing anxiously at her bedside. She looks up at them and smiles wanly. "A piece of cake," she says.

"They got nine eggs!" Eve says excitedly. "Can you imagine? Nine!"

"It would make a helluva omelette," Marilyn says. "Sweetie, will you see if they've got any brandy. I could do with a drink."

By four-thirty, after a checkup by Dr. Primster, she is pronounced able to return home, and the two other women help her dress. The bandage over her incisions is remarkably small.

"Have you got a back door to this place?" Marilyn asks Primster. "Just in case those groupies are still waiting. I'm in no mood to sign autographs."

He assures her that there is a rear door leading to a courtyard. After crossing that, they can enter the back entrance of a small office building and eventually exit onto 69th Street.

"My favorite number," Marilyn says. "Harry, call the limo and have it meet us there. I want to go home! I feel like I can sleep for a week."

The women depart, and in front of the clinic, on 70th Street, Ronald Yates paces up and down, waiting for the reappearance of his darling.

He sees the building empty out, the lights go off, darkness fills the city streets. He reckons he has been fired, but he is not worried about losing his job. He has a scroll at home naming him Yum-Yum's "Speediest Burger Flipper of the Year (Northeast Region)," and he knows that with his spatula dexterity, any fast-food joint would be happy to hire him.

He decides he will continue his watch for a few more hours. Then, if Marilyn doesn't appear, he will drive home to Staten Island, stopping en route to pick up a take-out dinner for his mother.

The street is deserted now, only one lighted window in the building Marilyn entered. A few minutes after ten o'clock, a green Chevy, at least five years old, pulls into the No Parking zone in front of the clinic. Two men get out, look around casually, then march up to the door and knock. They are admitted almost instantly.

Yates, watching from across the street, is puzzled. The two men look like working stiffs, short and burly. One is bald, one is chewing on an unlighted cigar, and both wear clothes that the Salvation Army would reject. Ronnie can't figure what two nothings like that are doing in the same building with the world's most famous actress.

It can't be more than a half hour when the two men come out again. Now one of them is carrying what looks like a white plastic pail. Ronnie, curious, crosses the street, fishing a pack of cigarettes from his pocket. He doesn't really enjoy smoking, but it's the brand *she* smokes.

"Hey," he calls, "one of you guys got a match?"

They're so startled that baldy almost drops the pail. Then they recover, and the one with the cigar hands Yates a book of matches.

"Here y'are, kid," he says. "You can keep those; I got more."

"Thank you very much," Ronnie says politely and moves off down the street.

When he stops and looks back, they're putting the pail in the trunk of the Chevy. He watches them lock the trunk, then get into the car and drive away.

He returns to his Volkswagen. But before he starts the long drive home, he examines the book of matches the guy gave him. It's a cheap job: crude black printing on white.

Turk's Bar & Grill. Atlantic Avenue. Brooklyn.

Manhattan, NY

Pawning his wife's wedding ring has brought Sam Davidson to a fleabag hotel in Times Square. Its musty lobby is crowded with what appears to be the entire cast of *Guys and Dolls,* plus a few extra hookers, crack dealers, and one guy selling "Jesus Saves" buttons at two bucks a pop. Sam remembers when he used to stay at the Plaza. But that was when he had more than $43.78 in his poke.

Sitting gingerly on the edge of the ratty bed, Sam flips through his little black address book and tries to find someone in New York he can put the bite on. He figures he needs at least a G, but he'll settle for five yards, or even two, or even some walking-around money.

The first dozen calls he makes aren't encouraging. No answer, or the phone's been disconnected, or the guy at the other end hangs up the moment Sam identifies himself. He really can't blame them; he's stiffed so many people; the word has spread from coast to coast that Davidson is on his uppers and strictly bad news.

Finally, scraping the bottom of the barrel, he comes across the names of Louella and Loretta Chin. They are attractive Chinese-American twins who once starred in a Golden Stream epic Sam produced titled *Two from Column P.* The last he heard of the Chin twins, they had moved to Manhattan and had found a sugar daddy who pays all their bills, lets them freelance on Central Park South, and never demands a cut of their take.

Sam calls the number, keeping his fingers crossed. The man's voice that answers is high-pitched and lispy. "The DuBois residence," he says.

"I'm trying to locate Louella and Loretta Chin," Sam says, "and I was hoping you might be able to help me."

"Jus' a moment, pliz," the guy says.

Sam waits, and then a woman comes on the line.

"Who's this?" she asks.

"Louella?" Sam says. "Loretta? This is Sam Davidson."

He's prepared for instant rejection, but instead the woman laughs delightedly. "Sam, darling!" she cries. "How nice! It's Louella. Where are you—in LA?"

"Nope, I'm right here in little old New York. I flew in for a few days on business, and I thought maybe we could get together, tear a herring, and talk over old times. Any chance?"

"Just a minute, Sam. Let me find out what the schedule is."

It's more than a minute, but he waits patiently. Then . . .

"Hi, Sam, this is Loretta. How you doing?"

"Surviving," he says. "I hear you girls fell in the outhouse and came up with a box lunch."

"We're getting by. Listen, Sam, we'd love to see you. But we have to go out around twelve—it's Saturday night, you know, and the mooches will be howling at the moon. If you could get up here right now, we could have like a drink together and a couple of laughs."

"Sounds good," he says. "Where are you located?"

"Park Avenue," she says, and pauses for his reaction.

"Mazeltov!" he says. "I'll have to change my socks. What's the address?"

He takes a cab uptown, willing to pay the tariff because he's certain he's going to score. He'll promise the girls meaty roles in *Private Parts, II,* and he figures they'll be good for a grand. Maybe more if he can convince them that it's going to star Marilyn Taylor.

The new apartment house north of 79th Street smells of money. The uniformed doorman is right out of *The Student Prince,* and the guy running the elevator is wearing white tails and a starched dickey. The corridors are muffled with mauve carpeting and lighted with ornate wall sconces, each little shade with a beaded fringe.

The interior decorators, Davidson figures, were from the famous firm of Glitz & Schlock, Inc.

An ancient Asian (Thai? Malay? Burmese?) wearing a gray alpaca jacket opens the door. He's the lisper and, with much bowing and hissing, ushers the guest into a living room only slightly smaller than the Waldorf lobby. Sam gets a quick impression of leather, chrome, and crystal, but then the ceramic dolls come scampering from a back room to embrace him.

They seat him in a sling chair covered with buttery calfskin and bring him a Chivas Regal in a Baccarat highball glass so heavy he has to hold it with both hands. They're drinking something green in dimpled glasses, and curl onto the floor at his feet, lolling on the hide of what had to be the fattest zebra in Africa.

They start twittering away about their kooky adventures with New York johns, giggling and choking with laughter, and he gets a good look at them. There's no doubt they're in the chips. They're wearing matching costumes: tightly-fitted black velvet jumpsuits with industrial zippers down the front. And their diamond pins, shaped like flamingoes, didn't come from Cracker Jack boxes.

Sam is about to steer the conversation around to his script for *Private*

Parts, II, Marilyn Taylor, and his current need for refinancing when a tall black wearing opaque shades comes strolling from the back of the apartment.

Slumped in his sling chair, Davidson looks up and figures the guy's got to be seven feet tall. He's built like a pencil, and he's wrapped in a burgundy dressing gown so heavily brocaded he can hardly bend his skinny arms. His legs and feet are bare below the gown, and he's got a dragon tattooed on his hairless left calf.

"Champ, this is Sam Davidson," Loretta says brightly. "Sam, meet Champ DuBois."

Davidson can't struggle out of that low chair and settles for raising a hand in greeting. Champ nods, moves to the marble-topped bar, and pours himself a cognac.

"Welcome to New York, Mr. Davidson," he says. "I hope you enjoy your stay."

"Thanks," Sam says. "Nice place you got here."

"Glad you like it," the other man says negligently. "But I do feel it needs a spot of color. I have my eye on a Picasso that would look smashing on the wall over that white leather chesterfield."

"A Picasso? That'll set you back a few bucks."

"Oh, I wasn't planning on buying it," DuBois says. "I'm a professional thief. Didn't the ladies tell you?"

Sam takes a gulp of his drink. "Why, no," he says, "they didn't mention it. A professional thief, huh? I guess there's a lot of money in that these days."

"There is indeed," Champ says. "But of course one must calculate the risk-reward ratio carefully. And what brings you to our fair city, Mr. Davidson?"

"I'm in flicks," Sam says boldly, "and I winged in to wrap up a new project. Dynamite script. A real grosser. I'm hoping to get Marilyn Taylor to star."

"Oh? That does sound interesting. I'd like to hear more about it." DuBois pauses to glance down at his gold Rolex. "Time, ladies," he calls to the Chin twins. "Your clients will be getting anxious. Run along now. I'll be happy to entertain our guest."

Chattering nonstop, Louella and Loretta rush into a back room and emerge a moment later with identical white mink stoles and black alligator shoulderbags. They kiss Champ and Sam good-night and go skipping out the door, still nattering.

"Lovely girls," Sam offers.

"They surely are," DuBois agrees. "And so wonderfully brainless." He coils his lanky frame into a deep tub chair facing Sam. "I have a small confession to make to you, Mr. Davidson. My name is not really Champ DuBois. It is Moses Leroy Washington. But I never felt like a Moses or a Leroy—even as a youth—so I selected a name I felt more in keeping with my personality and aspirations."

Sam stares at him, wondering if the guy's putting him on—or maybe he's stoned. But he can't see the eyes behind those dark sunglasses, and DuBois hasn't smiled yet.

"That's okay," he says. "You're entitled to call yourself any name you like. Champ DuBois sounds good to me. Like a riverboat gambler."

"Precisely," the host says. "I see you need a refill. I'm afraid our houseman has retired for the evening. Please help yourself."

"Sure," Sam says, struggling out of his chair. He pours a fresh drink at the bar, noting the crystal ice bucket, Baccarat glasses, onyx ashtrays, and a sterling silver cocktail shaker with an engraved monogram: KLR.

"Are you interested in movies, Mr. DuBois?" he asks.

"Very much so. At one time I had ambitions to become an actor, but because of my color and height I found the opportunities for employment were nonexistent. So I adopted another vocation. But I am still interested in the silver screen. So tell me more about this new film of yours, Mr. Davidson. I am fascinated by the creative process."

Sam explains that he was the producer of *Private Parts,* the movie that made Marilyn Taylor a star. Now he has a blockbuster script for a sequel, and he's come to New York to persuade Marilyn to accept the leading role.

"It's about this librarian," he says earnestly. "Very square and mousy. You wouldn't know she's beautiful until the first bed scene when she takes off her glasses. Anyway, she's got a stinker for a father, a widower and a real no-goodnik who keeps her under his thumb so she can be his cook and housekeeper and all. A little bit of incest there, too. Then one day this guy shows up, a real macho type, to clean out their septic tank. And he opens her up—you know? Teaches her how to rub the bacon, and it's a whole new ballgame for her. So they plot to off the old man. But she double-crosses the stud, and he gets the gas chamber for the kill. She inherits and is living on top of the world, screwing up a storm and all, but then the ghosts of the stud and her dear old dad come back to haunt her. The film ends with her being carted off to the loony bin. That's just the bare bones of the story, but I tell you it's real Oscar material—absolutely explosive. But it needs Marilyn Taylor to carry it."

"Yes, I can understand that," DuBois says thoughtfully. "She is a woman of talent, taste, and refinement. A close friend of yours?"

"Oh, yeah," Sam says. "The closest."

"Then you probably know that she has amassed one of the world's finest private collections of jewels. I speak now of first-rate pieces, some of historical importance. For instance, I happen to know that last year she bought at auction—anonymously, of course—a forty-carat marquise-cut yellow diamond, flawless, that had originally been owned by Ivan the Terrible or Hugh the Great—I forget which. In any event, it is said she paid almost two million for the stone."

"Well," Sam says, trying to laugh, "diamonds are a girl's best friend."

"Then she has many friends," his host says broodingly. "Many. You intend to see her personally while you're in town?"

"I hope to, yes," Davidson says, suddenly not at all happy about the way this conversation is going.

"At her home?"

"I suppose so."

"Would it be possible for me to meet her? Briefly, of course. I've admired her for many years."

"I don't know," Sam says cautiously. "Maybe it could be arranged."

Then there is silence. Davidson tries to return the other man's stare, but it's difficult to focus his gaze on those reflective disks of dark glasses.

"I would be willing to reimburse you for your trouble," Champ says quietly. "A finder's fee, so to speak."

"And all you want to do is meet her?"

"That's all. But it must be at her home. It would be worth a thousand to me."

"I'll try to work it," Sam says hoarsely. "No guarantee."

"I think the game is worth the candle," DuBois says. "Excuse me a moment."

He goes into an inner room and comes out a few moments later with a white envelope.

"A thousand," he says. "In fifties. Used bills. Just for a short visit to Marilyn Taylor's home. As soon as possible. Please don't disappoint me."

"I'll get on it the first thing Monday morning," Sam says.

"Good. And keep in touch. I would not care to come looking for you."

Champ DuBois smiles for the first time, and Sam Davidson wishes he hadn't. It reminds him of that shark in *Jaws.*

Manhattan, NY

The call comes to the East 63rd Street town house a little after 6:00 A.M. on Sunday morning. Harriet, a light sleeper, picks up on the second ring.

"H'lo?" she says.

"Is this Marilyn Taylor's residence?" A man's voice. Squeaky.

"Do you know what time it is?" Harriet says indignantly. "Who are you and what do you want?"

"This is Doctor Reginald Primster. May we speak to Marilyn Taylor please. This is an emergency."

Harriet swings her legs out of bed, reaches for a cigarette. "This is her secretary. Marilyn is sleeping, and I'm not going to disturb her until you tell me what this is all about."

A moment of silence, then: "We are sorry to report that Ms. Taylor's eggs have been stolen."

Harriet snaps the cigarette in trembling fingers. "WHAT!"

"The institute was robbed last night around ten o'clock. The only person present was a laboratory technician. He was overpowered and tied up. The watchman came on duty at midnight and found him. We were called and went immediately to the clinic. We are calling from there now. We have just finished a complete inventory, and apparently the only thing taken was the refrigerator flask containing Ms. Taylor's eggs."

"Oh, Jesus," Harriet says despairingly. "Have you called the cops?"

"No, we have not," Primster says, trying to keep his voice steady. "We thought it best to inform Ms. Taylor first to determine what action she wishes me to take. We can't tell you how shocked and outraged we are. To our knowledge, it is the first time a fertility clinic has been robbed. It is so senseless. What on earth can the motive possibly be?"

"Money," the secretary says promptly. "She's got it, and they want it. This is a kidnapping, doc. Listen, I think you better get your ass over here pronto. I'll wake Marilyn up and fill her in on what's happened. When you get here, we'll talk about what to do next."

She hangs up, finally gets a cigarette going, and dresses swiftly. Before waking Marilyn, she rouses the housekeeper and tells her to prepare a big pot of coffee and heat up some bagels, croissants, muffins—whatever's available. Then she goes to Marilyn's bedroom.

The Most Beautiful Woman in the World is snoring gently in an eye mask, ear plugs, and a Marilyn Taylor Nighty-Nite Bra, designed to prevent sag. Harriet shakes her shoulder roughly, ignoring the mumbled protests. Marilyn finally sits up, discarding her mask and plugs.

"Holy Moly!" she complains, glancing at the bedside clock. "It's practically yesterday. This better be good."

"Not good," Harriet says grimly. "Bad."

Then she tells the star what has happened. She expects a furious explosion, but Marilyn doesn't scream or curse. Instead, her eyes become hard and distant.

"Just my eggs? No one else's?"

"That's what the doc said."

"An inside job," Marilyn says definitely. "Who knew the eggs were there? Me, you, Eve and Eric Bannon, and Primster's people. Someone in the clinic talked."

"Probably," Boltz agrees. "But it could have been innocent boasting. 'Guess who we operated on today'—that kind of thing. Someone overheard it and decided to score."

"And hold them for ransom?"

"That's my guess. What else are they going to do with them?"

"The bastards!" Marilyn shouts, wrath finally escaping.

"Primster is on his way over. He wants to know if he should call the cops."

"No way. If we're right about it being a kidnapping, we'll be hearing from the gonifs, and we'll deal with them."

"Will you pay?"

"Sure I will. I can't disappoint Eve and Eric. And besides, goddammit, they're *my* eggs, part of my body, part of me. Oh, I'll pay to get them back all right, and after I do, I'll hire the best detectives in the world to find the shitheads who pulled this caper, and take care of them personally. Listen, Harry, I think you better wake up Tony Perez and Gary Flomm, and bring them in on this. If we're going to be dealing with hard cases, I'll need my bodyguard and his cannon close to me. And if we get any reporters nosing around, Gary might as well earn his keep as press agent."

"I forgot to ask," Harriet says. "How are you feeling? I mean, are the incisions giving you any pain?"

"Nothing I can't manage," Marilyn says. "I'm a tough cookie; I thought you knew that. Now let me get dressed."

An hour later they're all sitting in the big kitchen, slurping black coffee and gnawing warm bagels. Dr. Primster, eyes bleaker than ever, apologizes again, then relates additional details about the theft.

"The employee is Nicholas Kazanian, a laboratory technician. He has been with us several years. He is not a highly educated man, but very efficient and absolutely trustworthy. He was working late last night. Around ten o'clock he heard a banging on the front door. He went downstairs, and a man shouted it was a medical emergency, so Nick opened up. That is not unusual; we have had several similar incidents in the past. When the door was unlocked, two men pushed their way in. Kazanian describes them as young—mid-twenties perhaps—and apparently Hispanic. He says both were quite tall. One had a mustache, one a beard. Both were armed with revolvers. They forced Nick to take them to the laboratory and identify the flask containing Ms. Taylor's eggs."

"So they knew exactly what they wanted?" Marilyn asks.

"No doubt about it. After taking the flask, they tied Nick up and taped his mouth. The watchman came on duty at midnight, freed Nick, and they called us. That's about it."

"Shit," Marilyn says disgustedly. "I wouldn't say that joint of yours has the best security in the world, doc."

"Who could have anticipated a crime of this nature?" he says defensively. "Our frozen eggs, sperm, and embryos are valuable, of course, but only to donors and clients. They're of absolutely no value to anyone else."

"Don't be so sure of that," Harriet says. "The donors and clients will pay to get them back, won't they? I told you this is a kidnapping. We'll be getting a call or letter telling us what the ransom is."

"But no cops," Marilyn warns. "I'm not going public with this."

Primster puts his half-eaten bagel carefully aside. "Before you make that decision, there is something we have to tell you. The eggs are in pipettes suspended in liquid nitrogen. One of the characteristics of liquid nitrogen is that it evaporates. If the amount in the flask is not periodically replenished, the contents will eventually thaw."

They look at him with astonishment.

"You mean my eggs will spoil?" Marilyn asks.

"There is that possibility, yes. From Kazanian's description, the thieves who stole the flask are common criminals. We doubt if they know anything about liquid nitrogen."

"Oh God," Harriet says. "That tears it."

"The only solution, as we see it," says Dr. Primster, "is to make a public announcement of the theft. And in your statement to the press, emphasize that the liquid nitrogen in the stolen flask must be continually topped off if the eggs are to survive."

Marilyn ponders a moment. "You figure the crooks will hear about it on TV or read it in the papers and keep the flask filled?"

"It's our only chance," the doctor says. "We hope they realize that if they allow the eggs to spoil, they will have nothing of value to sell back to you."

"All right," Marilyn says, "let's run with it. Gary!"

Flomm leaps up from his bagel and stands at attention. "Ma'am?" he says.

"Talk to the PR people from Merchandise. Write a statement—no longer than a page—to be released to the media. Get my okay before it's distributed. Call the papers, radio, television—everyone. Schedule a conference for this afternoon, early enough so we can make the evening network news. Try to get me on the *Today* show tomorrow morning, and arrange interviews with Donahue, Oprah, Walters, and anyone else you can think of. Have I forgotten anything, Harry?"

"A reward," the secretary says.

"Right! Gary, buy full pages in the *Times, Newsday, Post,* and *News.* I'll pay a hundred thousand dollars for the prompt return of my eggs, no question asked. And I'll offer the hundred grand to anyone providing information leading to the recovery of the eggs."

"You'll have to call the cops," Flomm says.

"Let me handle that. Harriet, call Roche on the coast and have him fly in as soon as possible. And wake up Loretta, Shari, and Sidney. I want to start planning what I'll wear at the press conference."

"Something conservative and sincere," Flomm suggests.

"I can do sincere, buster," Marilyn says. "I'll play it like that courtroom scene in *The Innocent Sinner.* Doc, I'll want you standing by to answer any technical or medical questions. Okay?"

"Of course," Primster says. "We shall be happy to assist."

"And Tony," she says to her bodyguard, "oil up your shooter and stick close to me. I've got a feeling that reward offer will bring a lot of bedbugs out of the woodwork. Come on, everyone, let's get cracking. Thank God it's Sunday—usually a slow news day. I want full radio and television coverage tonight and headlines tomorrow morning. I want everything!"

The World

New York *News:* EGG HEIST HAS STAR BOILING!

New York *Post:* EGG THEFT MAY BE COMMIE PLOT!

New York *Newsday:* COPS SCRAMBLE FOR MISSING EGGS!!!

New York *Times:* Actress Reports Disappearance of Ova from Manhattan Fertility Clinic

The story of Marilyn Taylor's eggs swiftly becomes an international sensation. It drives news of the Middle East crisis, the troubles in Ulster, and the famine in Ethiopia from the front pages of the world's newspapers. And, through the wonders of satellite transmission, television screens from Australia to Greenland bring Marilyn's plight to the attention of concerned viewers.

> "Her tearful message to the thieves, 'Please don't hurt my eggs,' touched the hearts of millions."
>
> —*National Enquirer*

Most of her ardent adorers know nothing of *in vitro* fertilization or embryo transfer. But they have seen Marilyn Taylor's movies, have read about her private life in fan magazines, and have followed her successful financial career with happy amazement. Now, sensing the enormity of her tragedy, they respond with an outpouring of love. Extra staff must be hired to handle the cablegrams, letters, phone calls, and gifts—including two live chickens airlifted from a Yugoslavian farmer who apparently misunderstood the nature of her loss.

Tabloids in the world's capitals are quick to exploit the more sensational aspects of the story, illustrating their pages with photographs of the star in a string bikini or wearing a bathing suit of her own design called Two Stamps and a Band-Aid.

But more serious periodicals use the robbery as a lead-in for articles discussing the ethical implications of the new methods of conception. The writers are quick to point out the desirability of Marilyn's eggs, which presumably include genes that might transmit her beauty, talent, and business acumen. But there are problems. . . .

"Debate rages on dollar value of stolen eggs."
— *The Wall Street Journal*

Public opinion polls taken after the disclosure of the theft show that the great majority of men and women of all races sympathize with Marilyn and believe she has been the victim of a cruel and heartless crime for which the miscreants should suffer.

"Poll shows 73% favor death penalty for egg thieves."
— *USA Today*

The problems of the eggs' value and exactly what punishment might be dealt the perpetrators are much on the mind of Deputy Inspector Hugh K. Gripsholm during his first meeting with Marilyn.

"Look, miss," he says, "right now I don't know if the Department is investigating a misdemeanor or a felony. Can you put a dollar value on the eggs?"

"They're priceless," she says.

The inspector shakes his grizzled head. "Priceless don't wash, lady," he says. "Neither does sentimental value. You got to put a price tag on the eggs. Did the operation cost you more than a thousand?"

"Yes," Marilyn says, not having mentioned the tubal ligation to Gripsholm or anyone else.

"All right, so you can claim the eggs cost over a thousand, and so stealing them becomes a felony theft."

"Look," she says, "don't make a federal case out of this. I really would appreciate it if the NYPD makes no investigation at all. Just butt out. I'm sure the crooks will contact me, and I'll make a deal to buy back the eggs for a hundred grand."

"That's not right," the cop says sternly. "A crime has been committed, laws have been broken, and if the perps are caught, they should be charged and punished. The way you want to handle it, they collect a nice bundle for breaking the law and then waltz away. That stuff don't go. Sure, we want to cooperate with you, but this case is getting so much publicity there is no way we can butt out. Right now I'm getting flak from the Governor, the Mayor, the Commissioner, my mother, and my wife. They all want me to find your eggs. Well, I want to find them too, and nab the guys responsible for snatching them. But I'll need your help to do it."

"You'll muck everything up," Marilyn says wrathfully. "The villains will see uniforms all over the place and get scared off. The goddamn eggs will be lost forever."

"Listen," Gripsholm says, "how about this . . . I got a man in my detail, a detective lieutenant. He's young, good-looking, and he's a smart apple. One of the new breed. A college education and all that shit. Suppose I assign him to your file. He won't wear a uniform; you can tell the reporters he's on your staff. Meanwhile, he can be poking around to see if he can get any leads. Maybe your own people are involved—you don't know. And if the crooks contact you, this man can handle the payoff and get the eggs back and maybe grab the bums who pulled the job. How about it?"

"One guy?" Marilyn asks suspiciously.

"Just one. He'll have backup, of course, but you'll never see them, and neither will anyone else."

"And he won't wear a uniform?"

"Nope. He'll wear civvies, and he knows how to dress nice."

"All right," Marilyn says grudgingly, "send him around. What's his name?"

"Jeffrey McBryde."

"Is he married?"

The inspector gives her a wiseass grin. "Just to the New York Police Department," he says.

Los Angeles, CA

Mario ("The Nose") Zucchi is having his troubles. "Sometimes," he tells his wife, "I don't even feel like getting off the hay in the morning."

"Mario," his wife chides, "you've got to go to work."

"What work?" he says bitterly. "It's all falling apart. There's no discipline anymore, no respect. Now it's every man for hisself. Whatever happened to the old traditions? Right down the crapper—that's what."

Not too long ago Zucchi and his organization had a sweet thing going. They were into loan-sharking, extortion, numbers, prostitution, and had a number of unions signed up. Their income enabled the Mafia's LA division to buy into legit things like bars, restaurants, beer wholesalers, construction companies. They even bankrolled a couple of films and set up a production and distribution network of X-rated video cassettes.

The Man from Chicago was very happy with Mario's success, and told him so. But that was yesterday. Today The Man isn't happy at all, and comes out to LA for a sit-down, demanding to know why gross income has fallen off so alarmingly. Zucchi tells him.

The Mexicans and Asians are taking over the city, muscling their way into business activities the Mafia had once called their own. There is still money to be made from pot and heroin, but the newcomers have the cocaine and crack market sewed up, and from their enormous profits, they're opening nudie bars, porn bookshops, and kips stocked with teen-aged whores, both girls and boys.

The invaders are crazy punks who drive around firing machineguns into crowds of pedestrians just for the hell of it. They kill cops, blow up the homes of rivals, and think nothing of raping an enemy's wife or girlfriend in his presence before they waste him. They are totally out of control, have no loyalty to any large crime organization and absolutely no interest in allying themselves with the Mafia, which, after all, was there first and worked hard to purchase politicians and stay out of the headlines.

And if all that isn't bad enough, the new generation of Mafia recruits are zips. To them, "Our Thing" means "My Thing." They couldn't care less about omertà and they'll rat on their mother if it means making a deal with the DA. They are just not standup guys, and the fact that a lot of them are doing two lines of coke for breakfast isn't helping things either.

The Man from Chicago wags his head dolefully and says that things are just as bad back east, and he doesn't know what the country is coming to with all these foreigners taking over. But at the same time, he argues, La Cosa Nostra can't allow increased competition and personnel problems to put it out of business.

"We've got to find new sources of revenue," he tells Mario. "Maybe instead of the big score, we should go for a mil here, a mil there. Pretty soon you're talking big money. Like this thing with Marilyn Taylor's eggs. She's offering a hundred G's to get them back. That's a laugh. I happen to know she's a multi-multi, and she'd probably spring for a big M if she was squeezed."

"Funny you should mention that," Zucchi says. "The guy who produces our porn flicks knows her. He's gone to New York to try to talk her into starring in some meshuggeneh movie he wants to make."

"Yeah?" The Man from Chicago says, interested. "This guy—what's his name?"

"Sam Davidson. We're holding his markers. He's a real asshole. He's got about as much chance of getting that bitch to make a film as I have getting a dinner invite to the White House."

"Uh-huh," The Man says thoughtfully. "You don't suppose he snatched the eggs, do you? To strong-arm her into doing his movie."

"Nah," Zucchi says. "He hasn't got the balls."

"How much is he into us for?"

"Almost fifty G's. I keep him on the string so he keeps turning out the wet-dream films."

"He's desperate?"

"You could say that."

"Desperate men do desperate things. Mario, I think you should go to New York and check on this Davidson. Take a couple of soldiers with you, just in case."

"If you say so."

"Yes," The Man from Chicago says, staring at him, "I say so."

Washington, DC

The Federal Bureau of Investigation is headquartered in a structure with all the architectural grace of a three-hole privy. It appears to be more fortress than office building, and its brutish proportions hint of grim doings within, tight-lipped determination, and precious little laughter. Not necessarily. There's a supervisor on the second floor who delights in giving the hot foot to dozing agents.

Early on Sunday evening, lights are burning in a conference room where a covey of specialists has been hurriedly assembled. The meeting is chaired by an Assistant Deputy Director, and the sole subject on the agenda is the theft of Marilyn Taylor's eggs.

"This is a hot one," the ADD says. "I think everyone in the country must have seen her press conference on television. So far we've had inquiries from the White House, Justice, and from a dozen field offices. They all want to know if we're getting in on the act."

"So do the papers and TV networks," the Public Information Officer says. "My phone's been ringing off the hook. I even got a call from Interpol. What's our official position on this?"

"That's what we're here to decide," the ADD says. "The Director is playing golf in that charity tournament out in Palm Springs. He wants us to come up with a short statement we can release tomorrow morning. Lou, what's the situation in the New York office?"

His executive assistant looks down at some scribbled notes. "They haven't assigned an agent—yet. But they've opened a file and are trying to set up informal liaison with the NYPD. The locals aren't too eager to cooperate. Lots of headlines on this one, and they want them all."

"How are they handling it? Misdemeanor? Felony?"

"The latest word is that they're treating it as a felony theft."

There is a small, hesitant cough from a bespectacled supervisor: the Bureau's top legal authority. "I am not certain," he says gravely, "that felony theft is, ah, the proper classification of the crime. It is quite possible it may be, ah, a forcible felony since it involved the use of physical force and/or violence against a person. It might be, ah, argued that Marilyn Taylor was not directly the victim of force and/or violence. But it can also be argued that her eggs, an intimate, ah, product of her body, were the target of such force and/or violence."

The youngest agent present holds up his hand like a schoolboy requesting permission to speak. "Couldn't it be kidnapping?" he asks. "If it's a kidnapping, we take over the investigation under the Lindbergh Law, don't we?"

"The Lindbergh *Act,*" the ADD corrects him, "and it would become our baby only if the victim is not released within twenty-four hours. After that, there's the presumption that the victim has been transported in interstate or foreign commerce. But *is* it a kidnapping? Bernie, what do you think?"

"In common law, kidnapping is the, ah, forcible abduction of a person against his will. Usually, but not always, kidnapping is accompanied by a demand for ransom. But the, ah, crucial distinction here is that kidnapping must involve the abduction or carrying away of a *person.* Whether or not a living but apparently unfertilized human egg could be so considered, ah, the deponent knoweth not. To my knowledge, the question has never arisen before."

"Shit," the ADD says. "I think we better get an outside legal opinion. I'd like to see the Bureau play an important part in this investigation, but we'll need airtight justification before we get involved. Bernie, what's the name of that professor of law up at Harvard—the old fart we've consulted before on tricky questions."

"Ah, I presume you're referring to Professor T. Hiram Farthingale. Top authority. Keen legal brain. He's retired now, but I'm sure he'd be, ah, willing to give us the benefit of his thoughts on the subject."

"Good. Why don't you give him a call—no, better yet, shuttle to Boston and explain the case to him. Let's see what he comes up with. Meanwhile, let's get to work on a statement for the media. We'll say that we will only be observers until it is determined if any federal laws have been broken. If they have, then we intend to play a major role in the investigation. That'll let the NYPD know that we're looking over their shoulder. This is going to be a humongous story, and we don't want the Bureau left out in the cold."

"Maybe," the PIO says slowly, "maybe instead of just passing out a statement, we should hold a full-fledged press conference."

"Good idea," the ADD says. "And don't forget to say that the Director is leaving a charity golf tournament to fly back to Washington and take personal command of the Bureau's activities in the theft of Marilyn Taylor's eggs."

"Is the Director really going to give up the tournament?"

"He might as well. He got wiped out in the first round."

Manhattan, NY

Nicholas Kazanian is getting a scary feeling that he isn't a criminal mastermind after all. So far he hasn't panicked, but if his carefully devised plot keeps shredding away, he figures he might have to sell his Toyota and hop the first plane for Hong Kong—or anyplace that doesn't have an extradition treaty with the U.S.

He had assured Pincus and Abruzzi that Marilyn Taylor would never go to the police. But now the fertility clinic is *crawling* with cops, and Nick has been forced to tell his fake story a dozen times.

So far the cops seem to be accepting the scam, but who knows how long they're going to keep digging. On Sunday afternoon he watches them dust the lab for fingerprints, and he can't for the life of him remember if Sol and Joe touched anything other than the flask. That's one worry.

The second—the *big* worry—hits when he watches Marilyn's press conference on the portable TV kept in the lab and hears the star beg the thieves to replenish the liquid nitrogen in the flask so her eggs won't spoil. If there weren't a couple of cops watching the TV set along with Nick, he would have smacked himself on the forehead and yelled, "Stupid, stupid, stupid!"

Because he knows all about topping off the flasks; it's part of his job. That's why the doctors keep a storage tank of liquid nitrogen in a corner of the lab.

But Nick had been thinking of so many other things, the need to replenish the liquid nitrogen once a day had just slipped his mind. Now, he realizes that if he doesn't get to that flask in the trunk of Abruzzi's Chevy before Monday afternoon, as planned, those eggs are going to spoil and the whole caper will go down the drain.

He sweats bullets until the cops take off early in the evening and he's alone in the lab. Then he calls Abruzzi, hoping the police haven't tapped the clinic's phones, hoping Dumbo will be home, hoping the scheme can still be salvaged and The Three Stooges will cash in on what that TV guy called "The Crime of the Century."

Abruzzi is home, thank God, and before he has a chance to ask any questions, Kazanian starts speaking in a low, urgent voice.

"Don't say anything, Dumbo. Just listen and do what I say. I'll take that thing off your hands tonight instead of tomorrow. Okay? Just drive over to our usual meeting place at eight o'clock. I'll be there. Got that?"

"Hey," says Abruzzi, "what gives? You said she'd never go to the cops and now—"

"Shut up!" Nick says savagely. "Just be there with your car at eight."

He hangs up and starts working swiftly. He selects the biggest refrigerator flask he can carry and fills it with liquid nitrogen. Then he leaves the clinic with one final hope: that the cops haven't yet discovered the rear exit to 69th Street.

It's not until he's heading for Brooklyn in the Toyota, the big pail of liquefied gas on the seat beside him, that his shakes taper off and he can begin to plan the remainder of the evening.

The bar at Turk's is empty, but Pincus and Abruzzi are sitting in the back room, nursing beers. Kazanian can see by their expressions that they're really spooked.

"It's going like silk," he says to calm them down. "Just like I said."

"Like *you* said," Abruzzi says, glaring through his Coke-bottle glasses. "*You* said she'd never go to the cops."

"Don't get your balls in an uproar," Nick says coldly. "So she called in the cops—so what? I answered their questions, and they bought the whole schmeer."

"Yeah?" Pincus says. "And what about that business of keeping the flask filled so the eggs don't turn black?"

Nick leans back casually. "No problem," he says. "I planned on it, and I took enough liquid nitrogen from the clinic to keep those eggs frozen hard. I figured I'd take the flask now, Dumbo, instead of waiting till tomorrow afternoon."

"How come?" Abruzzi says. "You told us your brother ain't shipping out till Monday."

"That's right," Kazanian says, "but you got so antsy about keeping the loot in your car, I figured I'd keep it in my place."

"When you going to call the movie star?" Sol asks.

"Probably tomorrow."

"Listen, Nick, maybe we should take the hundred grand she's offering and let it go at that."

"Nope," Kazanian says. "That's just her opening bid. I'm going to ask for a million like I said. Look, we can always come down; that's easier than upping the ante. So we ask for a mil and maybe settle for half. That's not so hard to take, is it?"

They appear to accept that, and Nick waits patiently until they finish their beers. Then all three rise and start out. A guy seated at the bar in the front room stares at them. He's wearing jeans, a black leather jacket, and his long straw hair is greased back. They don't even glance at him, which is a mistake. Abruzzi might have recognized him.

Boston, MA

Monsignor Terence Evelyn O'Dell exits from Saint Bartholomew's Hermitage, a haven for retired priests, and pauses on the sidewalk to take a cigar from a pigskin case he bought in London fifty years ago. He cracks the tip carefully, juices it up, then lights it with a wooden kitchen match. He blows a plume of smoke into the night sky.

"Hello, moon," he says genially.

He begins a slow stroll toward Beacon Hill. "Try to walk two miles a day," the young surgeon said after O'Dell's triple bypass. "And," he added sternly, "no more cigars, no more brandy."

"Yes, doctor," the monsignor said humbly, and his first stop after getting out of the hospital was to buy a box of Garcia y Vegas and the biggest bottle of Courvoisier he could find. He figures that at the age of eighty-three he's ahead of the game and might as well meet The Man Upstairs in a jaunty mood.

The timing is perfect; he finishes the cigar just as he arrives at the home of Professor T. Hiram Farthingale. The professor owns the entire brownstone, having had the great good sense to marry a wealthy woman. When she died (what a grand funeral that was!) and Hiram retired, the five-story house began to look, and smell, like a slightly fusty men's club. It is now complete with littered library, cozy den, wine cellar, and a cook-housekeeper who broils the best mutton chops in Boston.

"Good evening, Bridget," O'Dell says. "And how is your rheumatism tonight?"

"Acting up, thank you," she says. "But I try to suffer in silence."

"The best way," he says benevolently, patting her arm.

Farthingale, clad in a worn velvet smoking jacket, greets him at the doorway of the den. O'Dell is happy to see that an opened cigar humidor is on the drum table between two leather club chairs. There is also a full, cut-glass decanter and two snifters. The old friends settle in for their regular Sunday evening confabulation with sighs of content.

"I had an interesting visitor an hour ago," the professor says, pouring their brandies with a hand that trembles ever so slightly. "An emissary from the Federal Bureau of Investigation."

"Oh?" the monsignor says. "Been flouting the Mann Act, have you?"

"No, Terry," the host says, smiling. "But in the past they have occasionally consulted me on certain recondite questions of law."

"I hope you get paid for your expertise."

"I do indeed. A consultant's fee. Not large, but appreciated, I assure you. It is good for my ego that, at my age and state of decrepitude, my opinions are still considered of value."

"Of course they are," O'Dell says stoutly. "No varicose veins in your brain, Hiram; I can attest to that. Shall we have our first cigar now?"

They both light up slowly, with murmurs of enjoyment.

"And what was the FBI's problem this evening?" the priest asks.

"Did you happen to watch Marilyn Taylor's press conference on television?"

"I didn't see it, no—having a blessed BM at the time. But there was much talk about it at the home. I gather the poor woman's eggs were stolen from a fertility clinic."

"Precisely."

"A dreadful act. Dreadful that they were removed from her body in the first place, and dreadful that they were stolen. I am sure you are aware of the church's strictures against the new methods of conception."

"I am aware. But the FBI has little interest in the religious or ethical significance of the theft. They simply want to know if, under the law, the crime can be considered a kidnapping. If it can be so considered, then they must become involved in the investigation under the Lindbergh Act."

"I see," O'Dell says, alternately drawing on his cigar and sipping his brandy. "And what did you tell them?"

"I told them I would take the matter under advisement, research it thoroughly, and render my opinion as promptly as thoughtful consideration allows. But in this case I am certain that my first reaction will prove to be valid. The egg theft cannot be considered a kidnapping since that crime presupposes the abduction of a person. By no stretch of the imagination can an unfertilized human egg be classified as a person."

The monsignor pours both of them more brandy. "Are you absolutely certain of that, Hiram?" he asks. "Admittedly an egg does not yet have a sentient existence, but the potential is there."

The professor smiles at his guest. "You cannot kidnap a potentiality, Terry," he says gently. "The eggs are not alive."

The priest stares thoughtfully at the other man. "Let us suppose," he says, "that some unfortunate fellow has a finger cut off in an industrial accident. Would you say that severed finger is alive?"

Farthingale ponders a moment. "No," he says finally. "It has no life of its own. It is an object."

"Now let us further suppose that the accident victim is rushed to a hospital, along with his detached finger, and, through the miracle of modern microsurgery, the digit is reattached to his hand and eventually becomes a controllable and useful part of his body. You will allow the possibility of that happening?"

"I so allow."

"In other words, what was formerly an object deprived of vitality again becomes part of a living organism."

The professor takes a gulp of his brandy, knowing where this line of reasoning is headed.

"But until it was reattached," he says, "the finger was insensate. Was deceased. Was, in fact, of no determinable value under the law."

"Then the law really is an ass. That finger was of great value to the victim who lost it. It was part of his body, his skin, bone, and tissue. Now suppose, through some strange circumstance, the finger was stolen before the surgeons could sew it back in place. Would that theft not be akin to a kidnapping? It would not be the abduction of a *complete* person, admittedly, but it would be the snatching of a portion of a person, a portion with the potential to live again."

"Ah-ha!" Farthingale cries. "Live *again!* That's where your analogy loses its significance. Marilyn Taylor's eggs have never known a conscious existence. They may respond to chemical stimuli, but they can't feel pain or respond to a thought."

"How do you know?" O'Dell demands.

"Know what?"

"That an egg can feel no pain. It may very well be a sensitive structure capable of instinctive reactions to the world about it."

"That's rubbish!" the professor shouts.

"The potential is there," the monsignor insists. "Can't you see it? A human female egg might well become half of an Einstein, Shakespeare, or Rembrandt."

"Or Jack the Ripper. I will not admit that the *possibility* of Marilyn Taylor's egg becoming a human being qualifies it as a person."

"A *potential* person," O'Dell declares, "and to deny it is to deny the preciousness of life."

A new bottle of brandy is opened, fresh cigars are passed, the argument rages on and on until the wee hours of the morning. Then a cab is summoned to transport the befuddled and beamish man of God back to the chaste environs of Saint Bart's. But not before he has embraced and blessed his groggy and goofily grinning host.

Manhattan, NY

Following Marilyn Taylor's televised offer of $100,000 for the return of her eggs, more than a score of phone calls are received at the 63rd Street town house and several letters are pushed under the front door. All callers and writers claim to be in possession of the eggs and demand to know when and how they may receive the reward.

"This is just the beginning," says Detective Lieutenant Jeffrey McBryde. "Every hustler in New York will have a go."

"So how do we handle it?" Marilyn asks.

The detective flips through the pages of his notebook. "Dr. Primster gave me a very detailed description of the refrigerator flask containing your eggs: size, color, shape, manufacturer's label, and the identification applied to the side of the flask by the fertility clinic. If we ask each caller to describe the flask, we can figure out pretty quickly if he's just a flake trying to pull a con."

"You think of everything," she says admiringly.

"Yes," he says, "I do."

They are sitting in the town-house living room on Monday morning, drinking black coffee and nibbling croissants. The cop reminds Marilyn of a young Gary Cooper, but much more articulate. And so self-assured that she'd like to goose him. His boss, Deputy Inspector Hugh K. Gripsholm, may think McBryde "dresses nice," but, to her, the lieutenant dresses like an apprentice mortician.

But he's got sky-blue eyes; that's a plus.

"Now then," he says, consulting the pages of his little notebook, "according to your statement, the only people who knew you were donating your eggs were yourself; your secretary, Harriet Boltz; Eve and Eric Bannon; and the personnel of the Primster Fertility Institute. Is that correct?"

"Yep."

"Uh-huh," he says, staring at her thoughtfully. "I think I'll talk to Ms. Boltz and the Bannons."

"What for?"

"To determine their whereabouts at the time of the theft."

"That's stupid," she says. "Harriet and Eve and Eric have absolutely no reason in the world to snatch my eggs. They're as heartbroken about it as I am."

"I'll check them out, anyway," he says. "Just in case. By the way, where were you at ten o'clock Saturday night?"

She glares at him. "My God, you don't think I'd swipe my own eggs, do you?"

"It wouldn't be the first time a public figure faked a theft for the sake of publicity."

"Well, for your information, buster, at ten o'clock Saturday night I was right here in bed, sleeping off the effects of my anesthesia."

"You could have hired the thieves."

She shakes her head in wonderment. "You're a pisser, you are." She reaches for her pack of cigarettes.

"Please don't smoke in my presence," he says. "It's been proved that smoke from other people's cigarettes is also carcinogenic."

She slams her palm on the table top. "That does it," she says wrathfully. "I don't have to take this shit from you or anyone else." She jerks a thumb at the door. "On your way, sonny boy. I'll ask your boss to send me another flatfoot. You're canned as of now. How do you like them apples?"

"Exceedingly," he says. He rises and stows his notebook away in his jacket pocket. "You've made my day, Ms. Taylor. Thank you very much. I have more important work to do than track down your ridiculous eggs." He starts for the door.

"Now just wait one effing minute," she says hastily. "Don't be such a goddamned hardnose."

"I didn't ask for the case," he tells her. "I was assigned to it. I can be reassigned just as easily."

"Oh, shut up and sit down," she says crossly. "I won't smoke in your presence. Satisfied?"

But he still stands, looking down at her, his face tight. "I'll stay on the case," he says, "if you treat me with reasonable respect. I am a professional police officer, Ms. Taylor; I am not one of your wetbrained fans."

"All right, all right," she says testily, "you've made your point. Now sit down and relax."

Grudgingly, he sits at the table again. She pours him another cup of coffee.

"Are you always this touchy?" she asks him.

"Only when I think somebody's jerking me around."

"Who's jerking you around?"

"Maybe you," he says. "You claim you didn't start all this brouhaha just for the publicity. Then why are you doing it? You're a young, healthy woman. Next month you'll produce another egg. What's so heartbreaking about having those particular eggs stolen?"

She's been expecting someone to ask her that, and she has prepared what she considers a touching and believable answer.

"Listen," she says, "those are *my* eggs. They're my fruit. And I don't want a couple of scurvy no-goodniks maybe trying to peddle them on the black market or sell them for souvenirs. You're a man; I don't expect you to understand. But any woman would feel the same way I do—like I've been raped. I let a surgeon cut me open to get those eggs, just so I could help my best friend who desperately wants a baby. You think I'm going to let some slimy crook ruin that? Just the thought of a dirty stranger running around with *my* eggs is enough to push me right over the edge."

Jeffrey McBryde looks at her strangely a moment, then drains his coffee. "I admit I don't understand," he says, "but it's not important. All I need to know is that a felony theft has been committed. Now I'd like to talk to Harriet Boltz, if she's here."

"Yeah, she's upstairs. I'll tell her to come down."

"I want to speak to her alone."

Marilyn Taylor sighs. "God, you're a mule. All right, do it your way."

"I intend to," the detective says.

Staten Island, NY

In moments of high excitation, Ronald Yates becomes a mouth-breather, and that's what happens to him on Sunday afternoon.

He goes out around 3:00 P.M., to buy his mother's dinner: two barbecued chickens, a pound of macaroni salad, three dill pickles, and a box of chocolate eclairs. He returns with this feast to find Mrs. Gertrude Yates staring at her gigantic TV screen and grumbling.

"They interrupted a wonderful movie," she tells Ronnie. *"The Creature Who Ate Osaka.* That Marilyn Taylor is holding a press conference."

He drops the food in what little remains of his mother's lap and dashes upstairs to his shrine. Inside, door locked, he turns on his television set and starts the VCR with a blank tape to record her appearance. He watches his Love Goddess avidly, and that's when he begins to breathe heavily through his mouth.

He doesn't completely understand all that stuff about egg retrieval, *in vitro* fertilization, and embryo transfer. But he does grasp the fact that his darling has been robbed of something she values. It's enough to make his blood seethe.

And what's more, he knows who committed the crime: those two bums he saw entering and leaving the building on East 70th Street. They were carrying a small white pail that was probably the flask Marilyn mentioned on TV. Ronnie fishes in the pocket of his jeans and comes up with the book of matches one of the guys gave him.

Turk's Bar & Grill. Atlantic Avenue. Brooklyn.

His first impulse is to call the cops and tell them what he saw on Saturday night. But, as it happens to all men, glands conquer brains. If he could recover Marilyn's eggs and return them to her personally, he would become a hero in her eyes. He'd reject the reward, of course; accepting money would spoil everything. But surely she would invite him to a private meeting. She might even spend an ecstatic evening with him at the Love Barn, a roller-skating rink in New Brighton.

Resolved to prove his fealty, he fluffs his pompadour and sallies bravely forth, feeling like the leading man in Marilyn's film, *Singood the Sailor.* That stalwart fought and defeated a gang of priapic pirates to rescue the star from an unspeakable fate and return her safely to her ancestral home in Toowomba, where she rewarded her savior with her hand in marriage and the second largest flock of sheep in Australia.

Brooklyn, NY

The transfer is made on a shadowed side street a block from Turk's. The flask is removed from the trunk of Abruzzi's Chevy. Kazanian places it carefully on the front passenger seat of his Toyota, after moving the big container of liquid nitrogen to the floor in the rear.

"Everything's copacetic," he assures the others. "I'll take it to my brother's place tomorrow. Then I'll make my call to the Taylor woman."

"Leave us know how you make out," Sol Pincus says.

"Of course," Nick says. "I figure she'll want to close the deal fast."

"The faster the better," Dumbo says. "I got a bad case of the shorts."

"Welcome to the club," Kazanian says lightly. "Talk to you tomorrow."

He waits until they pull away, then gets into the Toyota and starts to drive back to his basement apartment on Bergen Street. He is wondering how he's going to ladle liquid nitrogen from the big bucket into the flask containing the eggs. In fact, he is so engrossed with this problem that he is not aware of the battered Volkswagen tailing him, slowing when he slows, turning when he turns.

He's on Nostrand Avenue when suddenly the VW speeds up, pulls even with him as if to pass, then abruptly cuts in front of him, so sharply that he has to stand on the brake to avoid a collision. As it is, the two cars come to a squealing stop with the Toyota's left fender nuzzling the VW.

Nick leans out his window. "You stupid jerk!" he screams. "What the hell you think you're doing?"

A blond kid opens the door of the Volkswagen. "Hey, mister," he yells, "you're on fire! There are flames shooting out from the back of your car, right under the gas tank."

"Oh, Jesus," Kazanian wails. He scrambles out of his car, leaving the door open. He rushes around to the rear of the Toyota. He can't see any flames. Or any smoke either. He gets down on his knees and thrusts hand and arm under his car. He feels no unusual heat.

He climbs to his feet, ready to read the riot act to that blond kid. But the Volkswagen is pulling away in a hurry with a chirp of tires.

"Hey!" Nicholas shouts, running forward. "You goddamned moron!"

But the VW is speeding away, so fast that he can't make out the license plate. All he catches is a big sticker on the back window. And the only part of that he can read is Yum-Yum—whatever that means.

Cursing bitterly, he gets back in the Toyota, figuring the VW driver is some kind of a weirdo who gets his kicks by telling people their cars are on fire. New York has plenty of crazy assholes like that.

He's about to start up again—but doesn't. He just sits there, stunned, looking at the empty passenger seat and realizing that the flask containing Marilyn Taylor's eggs is gone. Stolen.

"You fuckin' thief!" he howls in despair.

Manhattan, NY

Sam Davidson sleeps late on Monday morning, gets up feeling full of piss and vinegar. He's got a thousand simoleons in his wallet, and he takes it as a good omen. Also, Marilyn Taylor has been clipped, but good, and he derives a great deal of pleasure from that.

"What goes around comes around," he says aloud.

He dresses quickly, sniffing at his shirt and socks. He decides he better spend part of that grand on fresh clothes, enough to last him a week, at least. And maybe he'll check into a better hotel, some joint where the roaches don't hold a marathon in the hallway every night.

He buys the morning papers, then strolls uptown observing all the peasants scurrying to their nine-to-fives. The poor slobs. He'll rob a bank before he gets on that treadmill again. Just to prove he knows how to live, he stops at the Regency for a thirty-dollar breakfast, and while waiting for his eggs Benedict, he reads the newspaper stories about the theft of eggs Taylor.

It couldn't have happened at a sweeter time, he reflects, because now he's got a good reason to stall Champ DuBois. After he finishes his third cup of coffee, pays the tab, and leaves a lordly tip, he goes to the pay phone in the hotel lobby.

"Sam Davidson, Champ," he says brightly. "Hey, you don't mind if I call you Champ, do you?"

"Not at all."

"Well, I guess you heard about what happened to Marilyn Taylor."

"I am aware of it."

"I called her last night to express my sympathy," Sam says. "She's practically climbing the walls. Her apartment is crawling with cops, and every fruitcake in New York is phoning to claim the reward. I didn't think it was a good time to talk to her about the script or setting up a meet with you. Give her a few days to settle down, and then I'll make my pitch."

"Uh-huh," DuBois says. "The robbery has changed my plans somewhat. I think you better get over here as soon as possible."

"Well, maybe later," Davidson says. "I've got a full plate today—people to see, things to do."

"As soon as possible," DuBois repeats. "Within a half hour. Will that be satisfactory?"

His tone isn't menacing, exactly. Just calm and flat. But all the more convincing for that.

"Well, yeah, sure," Sam says uneasily. "I guess I can cancel a few things."

"You do that," Champ says.

When Sam gets up to that stark apartment, he finds the owner dressed completely in white: white suit, shirt, tie, hose, shoes. Even the rims around his opaque cheaters are white. And he's drinking a white liquid from a crystal goblet.

"Chivas and milk," DuBois says, holding up the glass. "Would you care to try some?"

"No, thanks," Sam says. "A little too early for me."

"It's never too early," DuBois says, and drapes his lanky frame on a leather chair, sitting sideways so his long legs dangle over one of the arms. "This Marilyn Taylor matter—an interesting campaign. An inside job, of course; I'm certain the minions of the law are aware of that."

"Oh, yeah," Sam says. "They'll probably have it cleared up in a week or so."

"Yes," Champ says, "that is also my estimate. However, from what she said at her press conference, unless the thieves replenish the liquid nitrogen in the stolen flask, the eggs will die. Then they'll have nothing to sell back to her."

"Yep, I read that, too."

Those black shades are turned in Davidson's direction, and he can only assume that DuBois is staring at him.

"A hundred thousand dollars is a ridiculous reward," Champ goes on. "A lady of her wealth is good for a million. At least. Wouldn't you say?"

"She might spring for that," Sam says cautiously. "God knows she's got the loot."

"Interesting challenge."

"What is?"

"Taking the eggs from the thieves before they can sell them back to her or before they are recovered by the gendarmes. Think of what it might mean to you. I'm sure that, in gratitude, she would consent to star in your new epic."

"Maybe. But I'm no detective. I wouldn't know where to start looking for the eggs."

"That shouldn't prove to be too difficult. Assuming the thieves watched Marilyn on television—a not unreasonable assumption—then they must now be aware of the need to replenish the liquid nitrogen."

"I understand all that," Sam says, "but what's your point?"

"My point, dear fellow, is this: Where would the thieves get the liquid nitrogen? Macy's doesn't sell it, I'm sure, or Woolworth's, K-Mart, or even a friendly neighborhood hardware store."

"Probably some place that sells medical and laboratory supplies," Sam guesses.

"Exactly. And if you could check the recent sales of liquid nitrogen in those places, you might uncover a very promising lead to the amateurs who have committed this fantastic crime."

"Hey, wait a minute," Davidson protests. "There might be a hundred places like that in the New York area. It would take a month of Sundays to check them all."

"Oh, personnel would be no problem," DuBois says lightly. "I can easily recruit a crew of clever, eager lads to make the actual inquiries. What I need from you is a complete list of names and addresses of the places where liquid nitrogen may be purchased."

"From me?" Sam cries, aghast. "Where am I going to get a list like that?"

"Oh, you're an intelligent chap, Sam. I may call you Sam, mayn't I? I don't think you'll have too much trouble providing the information I seek."

"Nope," Davidson says. "Include me out. I just don't want to get involved."

"But you are already involved," the other man says gently. "Can't you see that? You wish to obtain the services of Marilyn Taylor in your new film. Recovering her eggs will insure that."

"And what do you get out of it?" Sam asks boldly.

"The ransom," Champ says, showing his teeth. "Hopefully, a million dollars. With much less risk than attempting to purloin her jewels."

"It doesn't wash," Sam says, shaking his head. "Suppose, just suppose, I do get the eggs back and return them to Marilyn. She's so thankful that she agrees to star in *Private Parts: Two.* Okay, that's one thing. But where does the million bucks come in? I mean, she's not going to make my film *and* pay you a mil."

"I think she will," DuBois says smoothly. "When the eggs are recovered from the original crooks, I take possession and become, *de facto,* the thief. You act as intermediary. You are the contact between robber and victim. Only you can guarantee the recovery of the eggs. She pays the ransom in accordance with my instructions. The money is given to you for delivery to me. In turn, the eggs are given to you for delivery to Marilyn."

"It won't work. She'll never go for it."

"She'll have no choice. Not if she wants her eggs back."

"I don't like it," Sam says. "I've done some crappy things in my life, only because I had to. But I never ran the risk of doing time in the slammer. This is just too heavy for me."

"Too bad," DuBois says negligently. "Then I'll have to call the lady and tell her I paid you a thousand dollars to introduce us, and demand to know when we're going to meet. That should put the quietus to any hopes you might have of getting her for your movie."

Sam Davidson feels the vise tightening on his pelotas. "All right, all right," he says, groaning, "I'll play your little game."

He plods all the way back to that scruffy hotel in Times Square, with no desire to stop on the way to buy a pair of socks. All he can do is brood about the cockamamy plot he's ensnarled in and wonder how the hell he's going to put together a list of places in New York that sell liquid nitrogen.

His morning euphoria has evaporated, and he's in a vile mood when he unlocks the door of his hotel room. Mario ("The Nose") Zucchi is sitting on the unmade bed, and one of his apes is slouched against the wall.

"Hiya, shithead," Mario says genially.

Cairo, Egypt

The CIA agent code-named Ptolemy is the new boy in town. This is his first field assignment, and he's anxious not to muck it up.

"A piece of cake," Control assures him. "Your contact is a guy named Youssef Khalidi. I think he's a Kurd, or maybe a Baluchi. We call him Joe, and we've been using him for years. So have the Brits, Frogs, Huns, and Russkis. He's been on bhang as long as I can remember, and most of the time he's off the wall. But occasionally he comes up with a tidbit. We usually pay him fifty bucks Yank. Never more than a hundred. He's strictly a third-echelon canary."

"Okay," Ptolemy says nervously, "I get the picture. Where do I meet him?"

"The Coney Island Café," Control says. "All the cabbies know where it is."

"How do I recognize him?"

"He'll be wearing a green-striped djellaba and carrying a copy of *Playboy*. You can't miss him. Share a plate of dates and see what he's got on his mind—if anything. If you think it's interesting—fifty bucks. Sensational—a hundred. But no more than that. Stop by my hotel after you split. Now off you go."

To Ptolemy the Coney Island Café looks like a stage set from a Humphrey Bogart movie: beaded curtains, a three-piece combo playing atrocious jazz, a porcine belly dancer who moves as if she's overdosed on Valium, a smell of incense and hashish, and a mob of male American tourists in polyester slacks and Harry Truman shirts soaking up local color.

He has no trouble finding Youssef Khalidi; he's the only guy in the joint wearing a djellaba, with a copy of *Penthouse* on his table. Ptolemy figures that's close enough.

"Joe?" he says.

Khalidi looks up from his narghile. He's bearded and wearing square B. Franklin specs. "Effendi," he says, smiling and showing a gold tooth. "Please to join me. I am having arrack. Very tasty. Would you care?"

"Thanks, no," Ptolemy says hastily, having imbibed little but Kaopectate since his arrival in Cairo. "Perhaps a small bottle of Perrier. Can I get that?"

"Of course," Khalidi says, lifts his hand, snaps his fingers. A waiter is there immediately. Joe jabbers in a language the American cannot identify. "I am requesting that the bottle be brought and opened before your eyes, Effendi. If not so, then perhaps inferior water has been put into a used bottle. You understand? Now, do you wish to dine? There is a Coney Island Red-Hot. A sausage encased in a bun. Specialty of the house."

"Yeah?" Ptolemy says suspiciously. "What's it made of?"

"Ground-up goat meat, dates, nuts, figs. Delicious."

"I think I'll skip," the agent says, gulping.

"As you wish."

His bottle of Perrier is brought, uncapped with great ceremony, poured into a tarnished brass goblet. Khalidi lifts his tumbler of arrack. "May all your troubles be little ones," he says. "But you smile. Have I said something of humor?"

"Your toast. In my country it's usually offered at weddings."

"Oh? Why is that so?"

"Well, the bride and groom are toasted: 'May all your troubles be little ones.' Referring to children they may have."

"Children are troubles in your country?"

"Not necessarily," Ptolemy says earnestly. "It's a play on words, y'see. The toaster is hoping the toastees will have no troubles but little babies."

"So babies are troubles?"

"Relatively speaking," the agent says, his eyeballs beginning to glaze over. "But it's said with a humorous intent. It is not a curse."

"But why should children, a gift from Heaven, be troubles?"

The American gives up. "It's really not important," he says, taking a swig of his warm Perrier. "I'm sorry I mentioned it. Listen, do you have anything for us?"

Khalidi pushes his water pipe aside and leans over the table toward the agent. "Something exceedingly important," he says in a low voice, his breath smelling of malt. "Of such importance that I cannot divulge it unless I am in receipt of five hundred dollars American. I am enduring great personal danger by speaking of it."

"Sorry," Ptolemy says. "Fifty is my limit."

"Because I value my long and intimate association with my Yankee Doodle friends, I will reveal this truly fantastic information for two hundred."

"Tell you what," the agent says, "you tell me what it is, and if I think it's hot enough, I'll up the ante to a hundred. Okay?"

Joe sighs. "Effendi, you bargain like a used-camel dealer. Very well, here it is: You have heard what happened to Marilyn Taylor, your popular and beauteous movie queen?"

"Yeah, someone copped her eggs. So?"

"This I have learned," Khalidi says, almost whispering. "The theft of her eggs was planned and executed by a terrorist Muslim sect operating out of Beirut and financed by Iran."

Ptolemy stares at a new belly dancer who has taken the floor and is now gyrating to the rhythm of "When the Red, Red Robin comes Bob, Bob, Bobbin' Along," played by the jazz combo. The dancer's navel, he reflects, seems deep and capacious enough to hold a half cup of Nestle's Semi-Sweet Chocolate Bits.

"What is the name of this terrorist organization?" he asks.

"Do you speak Arabic?"

"No."

"Persian?"

"No."

"Hebrew?"

"No. Only English."

"Well, in English the sect would be called The Arm of God."

"The Arm of God?"

"Incorporated," Khalidi adds. "The eggs have already been taken out of your country in the diplomatic pouch of the Bulgarian embassy. They will be in Lebanon by tomorrow."

"Why does The Arm of God want the eggs?"

Joe rubs thumb and forefinger together. "For money, of course. Ransom. They will demand at least a million dollars American for the return of the eggs. They wish to buy Kalashnikovs from the Russians."

Ptolemy remembers a lecture he attended at Langley. "In this business," the instructor said sternly, "the outrageous is the normal."

The agent takes a deep breath. "All right," he says, "you get your hundred. I'll pass it under the table."

"I thank you, effendi."

"Now I gotta go," he says, rising.

"Wait, wait," Youssef says urgently. "You have not yet paid our bill. And do not tip the waiter more than a dollar American or he will not respect you."

Ptolemy cabs back to Control's hotel and finds his superior in the cocktail lounge. He is drinking something from a tall glass topped with a little paper parasol. The two men move to a corner table, and the field agent repeats what he has been told by Khalidi.

"Holy cow," Control says. "It could be donkey do-do, but it's so nutty it's probably true. This could cause an international flap. I better get a zinger off to Langley and see how they want it played."

"Don't forget to mention my name," Ptolemy says.

Manhattan, NY

Detective Lieutenant Jeffrey McBryde is reasonably certain that neither Harriet Boltz nor Eve and Eric Bannon had anything to do with the theft. But in any police investigation there is a drill to be followed even if you know you're just spinning your wheels. So he talks to the Boltz woman and then drives out to Scarsdale where he questions the Bannons. After that, he's satisfied that the three of them are squeaky clean.

Before he drives back to the city, he calls Sergeant Leonard Rumfry, his second banana, and tells him to pick up Nicholas Kazanian at the fertility clinic and take him to the precinct house, ostensibly to record and transcribe Kazanian's formal statement.

"While you're waiting to have it typed," McBryde says, "have the guy go through the mug books and see if he can identify the two bums who taped him up."

"A waste of time," the sergeant says. "This Kazanian is in it up to his asshole."

"You know it, and I know it," the lieutenant says, "but breaking him may take a little doing. I'm heading for Taylor's town house. Keep Kazanian busy until I check in with you."

On East 63rd Street he's told that Marilyn is busy at the moment, being interviewed by a reporter from an Oslo tabloid. So McBryde wastes time with Gary Flomm, the star's public relations assistant, going through the mail from crazies who claim to have the eggs and demand the reward.

"The stuff is all bumf," the detective says angrily, hefting the stack of letters.

"But you'll check them out, won't you?" Flomm says. "I mean, one of them might be legit."

"We'll check them out—eventually. If nothing better turns up. What about phone calls?"

"They're still coming. I ask every caller to describe the refrigerator flask exactly. None can."

"That figures."

"But it's a lot of work for me answering those stupid calls. Some of those weirdos give me a hard time when I tell them to get lost. Can't you guys handle it?"

McBryde shakes his head. "Haven't got the manpower right now. Look,

I know this thing is important to you people, but we have four or five homicides every day, plus umpteen robberies, rapes, burglaries, felonious assaults, and so forth. We're spread thin as it is. So if you can fill in for a few days, it would help."

"I guess so. For a few days. Hey, I've got to break up that interview. Marilyn promised the guy a half hour, and it's more than that now."

"Will you tell her majesty that I'd like to speak with her for a few minutes."

Flomm returns and directs him to the living room on the fourth floor. Marilyn is reclining full-length on the couch, talking on a fancy white French phone. When she sees the detective, she stubs out the cigarette she's been smoking and motions him to an armchair.

"I'm surviving, darling," she's saying. "I'm sure everything's going to turn out all right. Thanks for calling. It was sweet of you." She hangs up and winks at McBryde. "That was the president," she says.

"The *President?*"

"The president of Magnum Pathway Films, dummy. I'm not buddy-buddy with the White House, although I went there for dinner once. The gazpacho was warm and the coffee was cold. How you making out, sherlock?"

"Getting there," he says. "I wanted to ask you: How many people in Hollywood knew you were coming to New York?"

"Everyone," she says promptly. "I made no secret of it. It was in all the trade papers and gossip columns. Why?"

"Just wondering if there's a West Coast angle on this. Do you have any enemies out there?"

She laughs. It's a full-bodied, boob-shaking, jaw-cracking explosion of mirth. She even kicks her heels in the air. "Any enemies?" she splutters. "*Any?* Buster, I've got more enemies than Burpee has seeds. You've got to get in line to hate me."

"It doesn't seem to bother you."

"Why should it? I'm in a tough business. You try to be nice, and you get a stick up the nose. Tell me something. Do you always wear that same black suit?"

"It isn't the *same* suit I was wearing when we first met, Ms. Taylor. I happen to own four black suits."

"Exactly alike?"

"Yes."

"Beautiful," she says. "And I'll bet you wear boxer shorts and knee-high socks."

"As a matter of fact, I do," he says. "But I fail to see why the manner in which I dress should be of any interest to you, Ms. Taylor."

"And that's another thing," she says. "Will you, for God's sake, stop calling me Ms. Taylor? Would it kill you to say Marilyn? It's really very easy. Three syllables: Mar-i-lyn. Try it."

"Marilyn," he says in a low voice.

"Very good," she says, nodding approvingly. "When you go home tonight, practice it a few times in front of a mirror. Where do you live?"

"West Side," he says shortly. "Seventy-first Street."

"Alone?"

"Yes. Except for a cat."

"Oh-oh," she says. "Daddy warned me about bachelors who keep a cat. You probably have a spice rack in your kitchen and just love to make quiche."

He stands. "I have a phone call to make and things to do."

She gives him a twisted grin. "You don't like me much, do you?"

"No, not much."

"Why not?"

"I don't believe I've ever met a woman as aggressive as you."

"Aggressive?" she says. *"Me?* Sweetie, when I want to, I can be a pussy-cat—with emphasis on the pussy. My bedroom is on the fifth floor, one flight up. I'd like to see those boxer shorts. Maybe they've got little bunnies printed on them."

"No, thanks."

"Why not? I'm a good bang—or so I've been told."

"I'm old-fashioned," he says. "I think the man should make the pitch."

"Okay," she says equably, "make it."

Silence.

"I'm waiting," she says.

Finally he laughs. "You're something, you are," he says. "A barracuda."

"You sweet-talking sonofabitch," she says, rising. "You coaxed me into it." She takes his hand. "One flight up to paradise."

"Good title for a movie," he says.

"X-rated," she says. "I hope. Come along, sonny boy."

Her bedroom is a boudoir, all laces and flounces. The bed, big as a playground, is a four-poster, canopied, with curtains all around. She peels the comforter away. She skins down in nothing flat, flings herself onto the lavender silk sheets, and holds out her bare arms to him.

"Come to momma," she says.

She watches with some amusement as he undresses slowly and deliberately, hanging his jacket and vest on the back of a chair, folding his trousers carefully.

"Sorry I don't have any trees for your shoes," she says. Then, when he's naked, she stares at him and, startled, sits up in bed. "Gol-*lee!*" she cries. "How many women have you killed with that thing?"

"Oh, shut up," he says.

About an hour later, he slides off the sheets and stands shakily, looking down at her.

"You okay," he asks anxiously.

"On a scale of one to ten," she says dreamily, "I give you a twelve."

"Thank you," he says. "Now I've got to make that phone call."

"Use the one over there."

"No," he says, beginning to dress, "I'll phone from downstairs. Then I've got to get back to work."

"Oh sure," she says. "Now that you've worked your evil way, deflowered me, swiped my maidenhead, you're going to desert me. Cruel, cruel, cruel."

He swoops suddenly and kisses her lips, tenderly.

"What was your name again?" he asks.

She laughs and punches his arm. "Go play detective," she says.

He turns at the door. "By the way," he says, "I hate quiche."

He goes down to the living room and uses the white French phone. He calls Sergeant Rumfry.

"McBryde," he says. "Is Kazanian still there?"

"Yeah. He's reading over his statement before he signs."

"Did you put him through the mug books?"

"Sure did."

"And?"

"He picked out two Hispanics, one with a beard and one with a mustache. He swears those two hombres are absolutely, positively the guys who lifted the eggs and taped him up. I didn't tell him that one of his picks is doing five-to-ten at Attica, and the other guy was killed in a crack shootout two years ago."

"I love it," McBryde says. "Give me Kazanian's home address." He jots the information in his notebook. "Thanks, sergeant," he says. "I'm on my way."

Brooklyn, NY

Nicholas Kazanian lives in a scuzzy brick building on Bergen Street. Scanning the bell plate, Lieutenant McBryde sees his pigeon has the front basement apartment. The detective pushes the bell marked "Supertendint." Lousy spelling—but who cares?

A short, dumpy guy eventually shows up. He's wearing a sweated T-shirt, and there's a cigar butt stuck in his kisser.

"Yeah?" he says.

McBryde displays his potsy and ID. "I want to take a look at Apartment One-A," he says. "Nicholas Kazanian."

"You got a search warrant?" the super demands, talking around his cold cigar.

"Why, no," the detective says, "I do not. Perhaps I should go get one. It will give me the opportunity to inform Sanitation and Housing Inspectors that you have garbage cans out front with no lids, the light in the vestibule is inoperable, and from the looks of this floor, you have roach and rodent infestation."

The super sighs and swings wide the inner door. "This way," he says.

Kazanian's apartment looks as if it hasn't been cleaned or painted since Year One. There are stacks of racing forms and tout sheets all over the place, and the only decoration on the crazed walls is a framed photograph of Secretariat. The detective figures the guy has got to be a compulsive horseplayer—motive enough to pinch Marilyn's eggs and hold them for ransom.

In the stained bathtub, behind a shower curtain, McBryde finds a big container with a Primster Fertility Institute label stuck on its side. He uncaps it and cautiously moves his palm over the opening. He can feel the cold, and guesses it's liquid nitrogen. But there's no sign of the smaller flask containing the eggs.

He goes back into the littered living room and sits down on a spavined chair. Then he waits. He's good at that. He spends most of the time remembering those lavender silk sheets. He wonders if it was a one-time matinee or if it may be followed by evening performances. He reckons Marilyn will let him know. A ballsy lady.

It's almost an hour before he hears footsteps and then a key in the outside door. He stands quickly, loosening the .38 in his hip holster.

Nicholas Kazanian comes into the room, sees him, stops suddenly.

"What's this?" he says thickly. "Who are you?"

McBryde tells him and shows his shield to prove it.

"You got no right to be in here," Kazanian says. "It's illegal."

"I don't believe so," the lieutenant says calmly.

"While it's true I have no search warrant, I entered the premises pursuant to Section Fourteen-B, sub-section F-Eight of the Criminal Code. That allows entrance into private dwellings when the investigating officer has probable cause to suspect the presence therein of illicit objects and/or evidence of illegal activities."

It's all horseshit, of course; McBryde makes it up as he goes along. Kazanian looks dazed, and the detective marvels, not for the first time, how easy it is to con a wiseguy.

"Nick," he says gently, "let's sit down and have a little talk."

"About what? I just left the precinct house in Manhattan. I told the cops there everything they wanted to know, and I signed the statement. I even picked out photographs of the two bums who pulled the heist."

"Close but no cigar," the lieutenant says. "One of the guys you fingered is doing time in Attica, and the other one has been dead meat for two years."

"Shit," Kazanian says, and sits on his rumpled bed.

"Want to tell me who the two thieves actually were?" McBryde asks. Then, when the other man is silent, he says, "Going to take the fall by yourself, Nick? That's very noble."

"What fall?" Kazanian says indignantly. "I didn't do nothing. It happened just like I said."

The detective holds up a palm. "Please," he says, "don't waste my time. Just tell me why you've got a bucket of liquid nitrogen from the Primster Fertility Institute in your grungy bathtub."

"Oh, *that,*" Nicholas says. "I borrowed it."

"What for?"

"Uh, my refrigerator broke down, see, so I figured I'd put the container in the fridge with the lid off so all the food wouldn't spoil, see, but when I brought the liquid nitrogen home from the clinic, the refrigerator was working again, see, so I put the container in the bathtub until I could take it back."

McBryde takes two swift steps and yanks open the door of the ancient refrigerator. Inside are two black bananas, a package of greenish baloney, and four six-packs of beer.

"Yeah," he says, "it would be a shame if all that swell stuff spoiled. Nick, where are the eggs?"

"I don't know! I swear I don't!"

"Come on, make it easy on yourself. Return the eggs, and I'll try to persuade the Taylor woman not to press charges. You'll walk away from this with a slap on the wrist. But you keep fighting me, and you'll do hard time. You and your pals."

Pause. "We can make a deal?" Kazanian asks meekly.

"No promises," the lieutenant says. "But you tell me where the eggs are, and I'll put in a good word for you."

"I don't know where they are, and that's the truth. Here's what happened. . . ."

Then, hanging his head, Nicholas Kazanian tells McBryde the whole story of the theft, including the names of his two confederates. He relates how the flask was taken from the clinic in the trunk of Abruzzi's car, how he reclaimed it, intending to stash it in his brother's apartment, and finally how it was stolen from him by a blond kid driving an old Volkswagen Beetle.

The detective stares at him. "That's a very touching story, Nick. This blond kid—can you describe him?"

"I didn't get a good look. All I saw was that he had blond hair and was wearing a black leather jacket."

"Could you identify him if you saw him again?"

"No."

"What about the car?"

"Like I told you: a beat-up VW."

"Did you catch any part of the license plate?"

"No."

"Isn't there anything you remember about it?"

"Yeah," Kazanian says brightly, lifting his head. "It had this big sticker on the back window."

"A sticker? You mean a decal?"

"Yeah, that's it."

"What did it say?"

"Yum-Yum."

Queens, NY

Rocco Castellano hangs up the phone slowly and stares thoughtfully at his underboss. "That was Chicago," he says.

"The Man?" Vito Zivic asks.

"Yeah. A courtesy call. He just wanted me to know that Mario Zucchi is in town with two of his soldiers. The Man says it's personal business. Got nothing to do with the company."

"Uh-huh," Vito says. "You believe that?"

"Oh, yeah. Like I believe my Doberman can fly. What's so personal about Zucchi's business that he's got to bring two heavies along? It don't make sense."

"Zucchi's take is way off. You know Fat Tony, my cousin in Vegas? He tells me that The Nose may be asked to take early retirement."

"Where to—Forest Lawn? So Mario is on the skids, and now he shows up in New York where he's got no right to be, and he's traveling with a couple of enforcers. I don't like that one little bit. Listen, Vito, maybe you should ask around. Call your cousin in Vegas and also Dominick Nitti in Frisco. He owes me one. Ask if they heard anything about why Zucchi is in New York."

"Yeah, I can do that."

"The Man says Mario is staying at the Bedlington on Madison Avenue. Maybe I'll give him a call and invite him out."

"I hear he likes the sauce."

"He only drinks things that begin with an A. Like A vodka, A gin, A scotch, A brandy, and so forth."

"Like that, huh?"

"You better believe it. I'll get him loaded and see what he's got to say."

Staten Island, NY

Ronald Yates had intended to return her eggs to Marilyn Taylor as soon as he recovered them. But on Monday, with the white flask safely locked within his shrine, he finds himself racked by fears and fancies.

First of all, the police will want to know where and how he came into possession of the flask. Ronnie doubts if they'll believe his story that he swiped it from the car of a man he doesn't know. The cops will probably think he was one of the original thieves. He might even be jailed before he can prove his innocence. And his arrest will surely ruin any chance of meeting Marilyn.

More important is the way he feels about that shiny white flask and its contents. He can hardly believe it holds a living part of his darling's body. That realization is so awesome, so *intimate* that Ronnie blushes with the intensity of his sexual fantasies. He has a dried rose she flung away, a cigarette butt she discarded, and panties with her name embroidered on the seat. But now he has her *eggs!* The ultimate memento.

He removes the vented lid of the flask and looks inside. Liquid nitrogen doesn't scare him; he knows a little about it. A year ago he got a painful plantar wart on the sole of his left foot, and the podiatrist burned it off with liquid nitrogen. So Ronnie knows the stuff is probably sold routinely by medical supply houses.

Now, peering into the flask, he sees the level of the liquid gas seems lower than it should be. According to the newspaper stories, that means it's evaporating, and if he doesn't keep the flask filled, part of Marilyn will die. He cannot let that happen.

Yates is not totally devoid of street smarts. He figures it would be dumb to buy the liquid nitrogen close to home. Maybe the guy who sells it to him would recognize him from the Yum-Yum Burger Shoppe. Or maybe Ronald will have to show identification before they'll sell him the stuff.

He solves the identification problem by digging out the business card of that foot doctor who treated his plantar wart. Then he grabs his leather jacket and starts out. His first stop is at his local bank where he withdraws two hundred from his savings account. While he's in the bank, he uses their Yellow Pages directory to look up the addresses of places that sell liquid gases. He picks out one on Canal Street, gets back in the VW, and heads for Manhattan.

Manhattan, NY

Mario Zucchi gives Davidson a hard time in that grubby Times Square hotel room.

"Sam, Sam," he says mournfully, shaking his head, "I don't know what we're going to do with you. For starters, you leave LA without telling us where you're going or where you'll be staying. We got a big investment in you, Sam; we want to know where you are every minute of the day and night."

"How did you find out I was here?"

"Your wife told us."

"You didn't hurt her, did you?"

"Aw, Sam, we don't hurt women. She was so pissed-off at you for hocking her wedding ring that she told us all about it."

"It was for a good cause," Davidson says resolutely. "I came east with a movie script to show Marilyn Taylor. If she goes for it, I'm in the chips again, and you guys get your stake plus all the vigorish I owe."

"Uh-huh," Zucchi says, staring at him. "You didn't snatch her eggs, did you?"

"You crazy?" Sam shouts. "Why would I do something like that?"

"Maybe so you could lean on her to do your film."

"That's stupid."

"Have you seen her since you've been in town?"

"No."

"Talked to her on the phone?"

"No."

"And you're not in bed with the guys who lifted her eggs?"

"Absolutely not."

"So you might as well go back to LA—right?"

"Well, uh, maybe not right away. She's very upset about the robbery and all. I'll give her a couple of days to settle down, and then I'll hit her with the script."

"Sure," Mario says, still staring at him, "you do that. Maybe I'll hang around New York a few days myself. Scoff a little braciuola down on Mulberry Street—just like mother used to make. I'll be in touch, Sam. You can bet on it."

Zucchi snaps his fingers at his primate, and the two of them march out.

Down in the lobby, The Nose beckons to his second soldier who's leaning against a fake marble pillar, cleaning his nails with a penknife.

"Keep on him, Dino," he says. "He's upstairs right now, but if he goes out, you go out. I don't mean you gotta walk up his heels; the guy doesn't know you, but I don't want him spotting a tail."

"Where he goes? What he does? Who he sees?"

"That's it. Call the Bedlington like every couple of hours. If I'm out, leave a message."

"When do I get a chance to take a shit?"

"When I tell you. Lose him, and you'll find yourself back in Palermo peddling sorbetto."

Upstairs, Sam Davidson sits on the edge of the rumpled bed holding his head. He's been a hustler all his life, and can't foresee the day when he'll be able to relax and stop scrambling for a crust. But his present predicament seems almost insupportable. He's got that wacko Champ DuBois making threatening noises, and now he's got the Mafia on his neck.

Sam casts his eyes heavenward. "What did I ever do to *you?*" he asks plaintively.

He goes down to the lobby and finds a public phone kiosk. Chained to the side is a tattered copy of the Yellow Pages directory. Davidson thumbs through it, but can find no listings for liquid nitrogen, liquid gases, medical or laboratory supplies. He calls Information.

"I got a question about your Yellow Pages," he starts. "I can't find any listings for—"

"Just a moment, sir," the operator chirps, "and I will connect you."

A man comes on the phone with a voice so tight and strangled that Sam figures he must have hemorrhoids.

"May I help you?" he asks.

"I'm trying to find places in New York that sell liquid nitrogen," Davidson says, "but there are no listings in your Yellow Pages."

"Which directory are you using, sir?"

"I told you—the Yellow Pages."

The guy sighs like Sam is King of the Klutzes. "Read what's on the cover of the directory you're using."

So Sam reads aloud: "Manhattan Consumer Yellow Pages."

There's another sigh. "Liquid nitrogen is hardly a consumer item, now is it? I suggest you consult the New York County Business-to-Business Yellow Pages. Have a nice day."

"Up yours!" Sam shouts, but it's too late; the phone is dead.

He has to tramp all the way up to the Hilton on Sixth Avenue before he can find a copy of the Business-to-Business Yellow Pages directory. But it includes listings for liquid gases, refrigerants, medical and laboratory supplies. Sam tears out the pages and stuffs them into his jacket pocket.

It would be easy to go back to DuBois's apartment, toss the pages in the gonif's lap, and say something cutting like, "There you are, Champ. It's simple—if you've got the brains."

But, on second thought, Sam decides he doesn't want DuBois to know how simple it was. He'll stall him for a while, tell him it's a tough job but he's working on it. Maybe he can con him into contributing another grand for "expenses." He stops at a stationery store to buy a pad of scratch paper and a ballpoint pen. Then he returns to his hotel room to make his own handwritten list of liquid nitrogen sources in the New York area.

While he's copying names and addresses from the torn Yellow Pages, Dino is down in the lobby talking on the phone with Mario Zucchi.

"He goes up to the Hilton Hotel and finds a telephone directory," he reports. "Looks like the Yellow Pages. He tears out some of the pages and puts them in his pocket. Then he stops at a store and buys a pad of paper and a   Now he's back in his room."

"Yeah?" The Nose says. "That's innaresting. Listen, Dino, if he goes out again, try to get into his hotel room and see what's on the pages he tore out of the telephone book."

"You want I should lift them?"

"Nah, leave them in his room; I don't want him getting spooked. I just want to know what's on those pages and what he's writing in that pad he bought."

"When can I call it a day?"

"When you do what I told you. Then pack it in, come back here, and I'll buy you a steak."

"Yeah," Dino says, "a thick New York strip with a big bowl of pasta fagioli."

"You got it," Zucchi says.

Manhattan, NY

Marilyn is wearing tailored gray flannel slacks and a black cashmere turtleneck, cinched at the waist with a wide alligator belt. Harriet Boltz is wearing one of her frumpy shirtwaist dresses. They're in the conference room of Marilyn Taylor Merchandise, Inc., reviewing a designer's sketches of the next year's wardrobe for the Marilyn Taylor Doll.

"What do you think?" Harriet asks.

Marilyn tosses the drawings aside. "They suck," she says. "No pizzazz. Fire the guy. Listen, Harry, what would it cost us to get that new man in Paris—you know, what's his name, the one who did the backless wedding gown that got all the hype."

"Louis D'Artagnan?"

"That's the one. What would it cost to get him to design an exclusive wardrobe for the doll?"

"It would cost a mint."

"Screw it; let's do it. Send Shari to Paris and tell her to make a deal. Anything else?"

"Plenty," Boltz says, holding up a folder of documents. "But nothing that can't wait. I don't think you're in the mood for paperwork."

"You think right. This business of the eggs has got me counting walls."

"Want a drink?"

"Hell, no. I've been drinking too much and eating too much. Just nerves. This morning I was up a pound. Did you hear from McBryde?"

"Not a word."

"That sonofabitch. You'd think he'd check in occasionally and let us know what's going on."

Harriet looks at her narrowly. "You balled him, didn't you?"

"Harry, he's such a prig, so proper, I had to find out if he's human."

"And?"

"Is he ever! But maybe it was a mistake taking him horizontal. I haven't heard from him since. He probably figures I share my wonton with everyone."

Harriet sighs and hold a match for Marilyn's cigarette. "You're also smoking too much," she says. "You know what I think? I think you got the hots for the guy."

"McBryde? Are you out of your gourd? The guy's a stiff."

"You just finished telling me he's a stallion."

"On the sheets he's a stallion. Off the sheets he's a cold fish. If I never see him again, it'll be too soon."

"You want me to call him?" Boltz asks.

"Yeah," Marilyn says, "give him a call."

Manhattan, NY

"You believe him?" Sergeant Rumfry asks.

"Kazanian? Yes," McBryde says, "I believe him. Look, he and his pals aren't wrongos. Just stupes hoping to make a quick buck. I'm not sure their elevators go to the top floor. That story he told me has details a professional would never make up: blond kid, black leather jacket, beat-up Volkswagen, decal in the back window that says 'Yum-Yum.' Outlandish, I admit, but I can't see Kazanian creating a scenario like that. I think it really happened."

The sergeant frowns. "Then you've got to figure the blond kid lucked onto the eggs. Or he knew exactly what he was after and planned that your-car's-on-fire scam so he could grab the flask."

"Right," the lieutenant says. "And I think the second possibility makes more sense. Blondie knew Kazanian had the eggs, knew what they were worth, and went after them."

"So where do we go from here? You wanna rack up the three villains?"

"All that paperwork?" McBryde says, groaning. "Not unless we have to. Right now, all I'm interested in is getting the eggs back before they spoil. That's our first priority. Suppose you pull in Kazanian and his buddies and get their statements. Lean on them hard. Maybe one of them can give you a lead on the blond kid. Meanwhile, I'll—"

The phone rings on McBryde's desk, and he motions to the other man to pick it up.

"Sergeant Rumfry."

"Marilyn Taylor would like to speak to Detective McBryde. Is he there?"

"Just a minute; I'll see if he's around."

Rumfry covers the mouthpiece with his palm, leans close to the lieutenant. "The Taylor dame," he says in a low voice. "Wanna talk to her?"

McBryde shakes his head.

"Sorry," Rumfry says on the phone, "the lieutenant is out of the office. No, I don't know when he'll be back. Would you like to leave a message? Okay, I'll tell him you called."

He hangs up. "That was Taylor's secretary. What's the matter—she can't make a call herself?"

"When you've got the money she has, you pay someone to place calls for you."

"Like my wife keeps telling me: Money isn't everything, but it's better to cry in a Rolls-Royce than to laugh on a bicycle."

"She's got a point. As I was saying, while you're scaring the bejesus out of Kazanian and his clowns, I'm going to try tracing that Yum-Yum decal."

"Lots of luck." The sergeant looks at him closely. "How come you didn't want to talk to Taylor? She swings a lot of clout."

"I'll talk to her—eventually. But I don't want her getting the idea that I'm at her beck and call. She's not paying my salary."

"You may be passing up something sweet," Rumfry says, grinning. "Ever see her in a bikini? She should have a Yum-Yum decal pasted on her ass. What a bimbo!"

"She's not a bimbo," McBryde says angrily.

The sergeant's grin fades. "Whatever you say, boss."

Boston, MA

Monsignor Terence Evelyn O'Dell relaxes comfortably in the leather armchair and watches appreciatively as Professor T. Hiram Farthingale carefully pours brandy into their snifters. The two gaffers already have cigars blazing merrily.

"You know, Hiram," O'Dell says, glancing contentedly around the den, "your home is beginning to look more like 221B Baker Street every day."

The professor smiles. "Which of us is Holmes, and which is Watson?"

"Oh, you're the detective; no doubt of that. I'm quite content to be your chronicler."

"Speaking of detectives," Farthingale says, taking the club chair facing his guest, "today I received another phone call from the Federal Bureau of Investigation. It has become an almost daily occurrence. It's obvious they are most anxious to establish legal justification for joining the search for the miscreants who stole Marilyn Taylor's eggs."

"Understandable. That crime continues to receive an inordinate amount of media attention. Apparently it has aroused worldwide interest. Something of a cause célèbre. And what did you tell the FBI?"

"I told them my research is continuing."

"In other words," the prelate says, laughing, "you stalled them."

"Precisely."

"I suspect, old friend, that you have no particular desire to see this matter brought to a conclusion since it has provided us with so many enjoyable hours of good talk."

"Elementary! And not only good talk but *profound* talk."

O'Dell raises his brandy glass. "*In vino veritas.* As a matter of fact, I have spent more hours than I should pondering the conundrum of Miss Taylor's missing eggs."

"And?"

"It seems to me that you have not yet adequately refuted my original opinion. That is, those eggs, frozen or not, should be considered a live human organism and, as such, their theft might well be considered kidnapping under the law."

"Terry, I suspect you are concerned more with religious than secular law. I, too, have given the matter a great deal of thought, and no matter how devious your reasoning, I cannot admit those eggs have an independent and sentient existence."

"My reasoning *devious?* An unkind cut, Hiram!"

"For which I offer no apology. Let me suggest a somewhat similar situation. Please, help yourself to more brandy; the night is young. Now I'm certain you are aware that in the excavation of ancient tombs and ruins, archeologists have sometimes found seeds that are thousands of years old. Those seeds are apparently dried-up, lifeless little objects and, given no attention, would remain so for millennia to come. But—and this is a big *but*—it has been found that occasionally, when soaked and given nutrients, those old seeds have sprouted and become live and healthy. But if the tomb in which they were found had not been excavated, and if they had not been watered and nurtured, they would have remained desiccated and without vitality. In other words, similar to Marilyn's eggs, if you will forgive me for speaking of the lady so familiarly."

"It seems to me, professor, that your comparison proves the point I wish to make. The seeds, like the missing eggs, have the potential of life."

"But they are not capable of *independent* life. They require an outside agency to quicken them. By themselves, unattended and unnourished, they will remain lifeless objects with no rights or value under the law. Let's have another cigar."

"Let's. What you are doing, Hiram, is making a distinction between what is obviously alive and what is temporarily inanimate but has the latent possibility of becoming viable. I claim that no such distinction exists. Both archeologists' seeds and Marilyn's eggs have been granted God's Gift, the Holy Spark, the Divine Fire. Life does indeed exist in them, but merely sleeps until awakened to the glory of sentient existence."

"Terry! That's poetic!"

"I admit my speech tends toward the fulsome when my tongue is lubricated by your excellent cognac. But my prolixity should not obscure the truth of what I say."

Farthingale inhales the fumes of his brandy, reflecting. "I might be willing to agree with your thesis if Marilyn's eggs had been fertilized. Then we would be dealing with embryos, on their way to become a viable fetus and eventually to birth. I will certainly admit to the potential of a human embryo. But I refuse to admit an unfertilized egg has what you referred to as the Holy Spark or Divine Fire. And I can provide evidence that conclusively negates such a notion."

"Oh? And what might that evidence be?"

"A healthy woman may produce a single mature egg a month. If unfertilized, that egg dies and is shed from the body. If a human female egg has, as you say, been granted God's Gift of life, why does He allow millions and millions of such eggs to die normally each day?"

O'Dell finishes his brandy in a gulp and pours himself another. Then he takes a deep breath and begins his rebuttal. The debate grows fiercer. Fresh cigars are lighted, more cognac is poured, and the two jousters have at each other enthusiastically, voices loudening, gestures becoming more florid.

The monsignor departs Beacon Hill shortly after midnight and saunters home to Saint Bartholomew's Hermitage. He smokes a final cigar as he strolls, admires the night sky, and hums a tune he cannot quite identify. He finally decides it is either "Beautiful Ohio" or "Under the Bamboo Tree."

Queens, NY

The steakhouse is in Ozone Park, and when Mario Zucchi gets a look at the menu, he whistles.

"They ain't exactly giving the food away, are they?" he says.

Rocco Castellano smiles. "Don't let the prices scare you, Mario. There won't be no tab. I own the joint."

"No kidding?" The Nose says. "Jeez, that's great. I always wanted to own a joint. You do okay?"

Rocco shrugs. "It's no gold mine but it pays its way. And it's a good front for this and that. What're you drinking?"

"Chivas. Seltzer on the side."

"I think I'll stick to Soave. My gut's been acting up lately. Let me see what we got that's good."

He rises from the table, walks over to the small mahogany bar. He motions the bartender close.

"Soave for me, Paul," he says. "That Classico we bought. The younger the better."

"And what is your guest drinking, Mr. Castellano?"

"Chivas. Soda on the side. Slug him and keep them coming. I don't want to see his glass empty."

"I understand, Mr. Castellano."

Zucchi orders the 24-ounce sirloin with a double portion of spaghetti doused with olive oil and garlic. Rocco has a hunter's stew: chunks of filet mignon and hot sausage, shrimp, and mushroom caps in a red wine sauce, served over green noodles. Both men start with the hot antipasto. Two waiters attend to their needs, keeping their glasses filled, bringing more bread, offering fresh linen napkins, replacing used silverware.

"Nothing like this on the Coast," Mario assures his host. "Believe me, it's worth the trip."

"Thanks," Castellano says. "Going to be in town long?"

"A week," Zucchi says. "Maybe more, maybe less."

"Business?"

"I'm carrying a guy for about fifty G's. He takes off for New York, so I figure I better protect my investment in case he's dreaming of blowing the country."

"You find him?"

"Oh, yeah. He's holed up in a ratty hotel in Times Square. I'm keeping an eye on him."

Then they don't converse again until their plates are wiped clean with heels of bread. The table is cleared, the waiters serve espresso and a platter of fresh fruit. And another drink for Zucchi, his fifth.

"Jesus," he says, sitting back and patting his gut, "I musta put on three pounds at least. Great scoffing, Rocco. Thanks."

"My pleasure. This welsher you're following—what's his racket?"

"Movies. He's the guy who produces our skin flicks. Now he's got a wildass idea of making a legit film. And guess who he wants to star in it."

"Don't tell me Marilyn Taylor."

"You got it. Listen to this. . . ."

Made expansive by all that rich food and good booze, The Nose tells Castellano all about Sam Davidson, his script for *Private Parts, II,* and his nutty dream of getting Marilyn Taylor to star.

"I guessed he might have lifted her eggs so he could lean on her, but he swears he had nothing to do with it."

Then he tells Rocco how he had Dino, one of his soldiers, tail Davidson, how the desperado was seen tearing pages from a telephone directory, and how Dino later got a look at what Davidson was copying.

"Places that sell supplies to doctors, hospitals clinics, laboratories. At first I couldn't figure it."

But then Zucchi realized what it was: those places sold liquid nitrogen, and Davidson realized the lowlifes who copped the eggs would have to buy the liquid gas if they wanted to keep their booty valuable.

"Good thinking," Rocco says. "The guy's not a total asshole. He's going to those places to get a lead on the eggs. Then he's going to swipe them back."

"Right," Mario says, grinning and working on his sixth Scotch. "Only I'm going to get there first. I found the same Yellow Pages he tore out. Now I got my own list. I called The Man this afternoon, and he's sending a crew of guys from Chicago to help me out. With that gang I'll be able to cover more places faster than Davidson. Marilyn is offering a hundred G's to get her eggs back, but I figure she's good for a mil."

"At least," Castellano agrees. "I wish you well. It sounds like a heavy score. Hey, listen, Mario, I've enjoyed this get-together, but I'm going to cut it short. In about a half hour, I got a sit-down with some guys from Canarsie. Business. You understand."

"Oh, sure. That's okay."

"And keep me up to speed on how you make out with Marilyn's eggs. I think you got a good thing going there. I'll have my driver take you back to Manhattan in the limo."

Rocco waits until Zucchi departs. Then he marches into the restaurant's back office. His underboss, Vito Zivic, is waiting for him, watching the fights on TV.

"How did you make out?" Zivic asks.

Castellano stares at him thoughtfully. "Vito," he says, "I need all the Yellow Pages for the New York area."

Manhattan, NY

Sam Davidson waits a day—and finally buys fresh socks, underwear, and a shirt—and then calls DuBois.

"I was wondering what happened to you," DuBois says.

"Listen, that was a hell of a job you gave me," Sam says. "I been working my ass off putting that list together."

"But you've got it?"

"Oh, yeah, I got it—complete with names and addresses. Every place in the New York area that sells liquid nitrogen. But I had to grease a few palms to get it."

"In other words," DuBois says, "you want more money."

"It's only fair," Sam says. "To cover my expenses."

"Come on up, and we'll talk about it."

When Davidson gets to the apartment, he finds Champ sitting at the bar with that wizened Asian, the lisper who opened the door on his first visit. The little guy is still wearing his gray alpaca jacket. Both men are drinking Perrier-Jouet from crystal flutes.

"Meet Mutha," DuBois says. "He is not only my houseman and majordomo, but also my comptroller and chief operating officer."

"Hiya," Davidson says, waving a hand.

"Hello, mutha," Mutha says.

"Don't let it throw you," the host advises. "He calls everyone mutha—don't you, Mutha?"

"Yeth, mutha," Mutha says.

"Well, here's your list," Sam says, handing over sheets of his scratch paper. "Take good care of it. A lot of blood, sweat, and tears went into it. I figure I spent four bills, at least."

"Give him two, Mutha," Champ says negligently.

The majordomo takes a leather purse from his jacket pocket—the old-fashioned kind with a snap clasp—opens it and plucks out four crisp, new fifty-dollar bills.

"Better not spend them today," DuBois says. "Give the ink a chance to dry,"

"Ha-ha," Sam says with a laugh that sounds hokey even to him. He's not absolutely certain this lunatic isn't printing his own lettuce, maybe from stolen plates.

Champ hands the list to Mutha. "How long will it take?" he asks.

The comptroller scans it swiftly. "Two, three days," he says. "With six good helpers."

"Two days tops," DuBois says. "And make it seven good helpers. Davidson will assist us—right, Sam?"

"Whoa!" Sam says. "Wait just one fucking minute. My job was to get you the list—which I did. Our deal didn't include my making like a detective."

"But I'm sure you'll be willing to volunteer your services."

"Not me, Champ. I'm an inside man, not an outside man."

"Just for a day or two?"

"No way."

"Mutha," DuBois says quietly.

The diminutive houseman reaches inside his jacket, slides a small, snub-nosed revolver from a shoulder holster, places it gently on the bar. Champ, using a long forefinger (the nail manicured), swivels the gun around until the muzzle is pointing at Davidson.

"Do reconsider," he urges.

Sam raises his eyes slowly from that gleaming hunk of steel, but he can't see beyond the blacklensed glasses DuBois is wearing.

"Well, yeah," he says hoarsely. "I guess it wouldn't do any harm to help you out for a day or two."

"Stout fella," Champ says. "I knew I could count on your enthusiastic cooperation. Mutha, why don't you call in the troops, and we'll get this search organized. Sam, you stay here until the others arrive, and then Mutha will assign a specific area for you to cover. Correct, Mutha?"

"Ith correct," Mutha says.

"Would you care for a glass of champagne while you're waiting?" DuBois asks solicitously.

"No, thanks," Davidson says. "The bubbles make me fart."

"Then perhaps something stronger?"

"Yeah," Sam says, "something stronger."

Manhattan, NY

Detective Lieutenant McBryde has Sergeant Rumfry and four other warm bodies assigned to him in the quest for Marilyn's eggs. It's not much of a task force but, as Deputy Inspector Gripsholm said, "The Department has better things to do than go looking for those Popsicles, and if the Commish wasn't so hype-crazy, I'd file the whole thing in deep six."

With such a small command, McBryde has to do a lot of the legwork himself—which is okay with him. He hates being chained to a desk, and this case is giving him a chance to move around town and use the skills he's getting paid for. Like this matter of the Yum-Yum decal . . .

He calls Yum Yum Boutique, Yum Yum Hot Dog, Yum Yum Ice Cream Stores, Yum Yum Hardware, and Yum Yum Adult Videos. To all, he identifies himself as a police officer and asks if they have stickers or decals that could be placed in a car window, advertising their business. He hits pay dirt on his sixth call: Yum-Yum Burger Shoppes, Inc., with headquarters on West 57th Street.

The lieutenant goes up there and talks to the sales manager, a nervy woman who wears two Paper Mate ballpoint pens stuck in her gray hair. She shows him the decals they distribute to their shops and employees for display on car windows or any other place.

"Cheap advertising," she says, "but effective. We also give away baseball caps and T-shirts. You'd be surprised at how many young chicks want to wear a tight Yum-Yum shirt stretched across their boobs."

"I wouldn't be surprised," McBryde says. "How come I've never heard of Yum-Yum Burgers?"

"We're not in Manhattan yet. Real estate is too expensive. But we're in Jersey, out on the Island, five shops in Queens, four in Brooklyn, two on Staten Island. Try one of our burgers, and you'll be addicted for life."

"What's in it—hashish?"

"Something better: a jolt of garlic. But that's supposed to be a trade secret, so don't tell a soul."

"My lips are sealed," he assures her. "Could I get the addresses of your places in Queens, Brooklyn, and Staten island?"

"No problem. We're happy to cooperate with New York's Finest. What's all this about?"

"I'm looking for a blond guy with one of your decals on the back window of his car."

"Lots of luck. What'd he do—murder someone?"

"Nah. But he's wanted for barratry and usurpation of advowson."

He leaves her reaching for her dictionary and heads for Brooklyn. He spends the remainder of the day hitting those four Yum-Yum Burger Shoppes. At each, he asks the manager if he employs a blond guy who wears a black leather jacket and drives an old beat-up Volkswagen. Zero, zip, and zilch.

He drives home through heavy traffic, telling himself he can't expect instant results. Tomorrow he'll hit the five joints in Queens, and maybe his luck will change.

It's late in the evening, after a tasteless dinner boiled in a plastic bag, when he can stand it no longer. He phones Marilyn Taylor's town house, telling himself the victim deserves a progress report. But the victim is at the theater, and McBryde hangs up with the woeful realization that he's hooked; he might as well join the International Marilyn Taylor Fan Club.

There are women he could call who could drop over for a drink or two followed by fun and games. But seeking a substitute, he admits, would be demeaning to the replacement, to himself, and most of all to the infuriating woman with the loud mouth, long legs, and industrial-strength lust.

He tries to laugh at himself. She's famous. Talented. All the money in the world. Beauty that doesn't end. And he's a cop. So she threw him a matinee. Meant nothing to her. Probably does it all the time. The thrill of the stranger. An incident. Finished and forgotten. No significance.

But his rationalizing doesn't work.

"Hooked!" he howls at his startled cat. "Hooked, hooked, hooked!"

Staten Island, NY

Ronald Yates gets his job back at the Yum-Yum Shoppe in West New Brighton, and he isn't even docked for the days he was absent; the manager is aware of what an adroit burger flipper Ronnie is.

He is happy during his grease-splattered hours at work for he knows what awaits him at home: his treasure: Marilyn's eggs. That chilled white flask has become an icon, an object of worship. And when he carefully replenishes the liquid nitrogen from a three-liter container purchased on Canal Street (using a small soup ladle for the task), he feels he is performing a liturgical ceremony, keeping alive and consecrating a vital portion of The Most Beautiful Woman in the World.

He also derives a more mundane pleasure from his prize. The disappearance of Marilyn's eggs continues to dominate the headlines and television news programs. And in all the world, only Ronnie Yates knows their whereabouts. Possession, somehow, makes him special, a celebrity in his own right. It is an intimate link to his angel and the wonderful world she inhabits.

Other Yum-Yum employees, and even his mother, remark on the change in his appearance. "What are you smiling about?" they ask. Or "You sure look happy. Win the lottery?"

He would like to tell them what he has won, and glory in their astonishment. But he keeps his secret inviolate, and at night, alone in his shrine with Marilyn's eggs, he feels a spiritual joy that can only be equaled by that of a True Believer in the presence of sacred relics.

So intense is his rapture that he gives no thought to the future, how long he may continue to possess the eggs, and what their eventual disposition will be. He is content with the moment, having realized the ultimate dream of every ardent fan: actually *owning* the beloved.

So might an Arthurian knight feel who, having happened upon the Holy Grail, clutches it to his heart and weeps tears of thanksgiving and bliss.

Manhattan, NY

"Those fuckin' eggs!" screams Mario Zucchi. "If I knew it was going to be so much work, I never would have started this campaign."

But his tantrum is mostly for the benefit of henchmen assembled in his suite at the Hotel Bedlington. They're going to do the pavement-pounding, but The Nose wants to impress upon them how hard he has labored on the plotting of the caper.

Actually, the simple plan required only a few hours of scribbling. Using the Yellow Pages, he drew up a list of all liquid nitrogen sources in the New York area. Then the list was divided by neighborhoods. Now Zucchi has six smaller lists for use by the soldiers sent by The Man from Chicago to assist him.

"How you handle it is up to you," Mario tells his gang. "All I want to know is who bought liquid nitrogen since the eggs were swiped. Talk to the salesman or boss. Give them any shit you think will work, like you're a private eye working for the Taylor woman, or you're from an insurance company tracking a robbery, or maybe you're a reporter writing a story on the eggs. I don't care how you finagle it, just get the scoop."

"You want we should lean on them?" one of the Chicago thugs asks.

"If you gotta lean on them," Zucchi says, "then lean on them. Listen, this is a big-buck deal. And I, personally, will guarantee a grand to the guy who comes up with the names and addresses of the bums who copped the eggs. One thousand smackers. Guaranteed. Now hit the street."

The soldiers file out, carrying their lists. The Nose is left alone with the gorilla who's been following Sam Davidson.

"You want I should keep tailing him?" Dino asks.

"Yeah," Mario says, "I want to make sure he's not getting ahead of us. Where is he now?"

"Up at that Park Avenue apartment house I told you about. It's the second time he's gone there. I found out who he's seeing, but I had to slip the doorman a double-sawbuck to get the skinny."

"All right, all right," Zucchi says impatiently, "I owe you. Who's he seeing?"

"A tall dinge who dresses crazy and always wears black shades. His name is Champ DuBois, and the doorman claims he's an A-Number-One wrongo. He's supposed to be running a couple of hookers, and his butler carries a piece. The doorman says this DuBois is loaded. He drives a white Jag and hands out tips like there's no tomorrow."

"Yeah? What's his racket—full-time pimp?"

"The doorman says no. You don't make that kind of loot with just two girls. But the guy ain't straight; that's for sure."

"I don't like it," Mario says nervously, biting at his thumbnail. "I want to know what his connection is with Davidson. Maybe the two of them are after the eggs. I think I'll give Rocco Castellano a call and find out if he ever heard of this Champ DuBois. If he hasn't, maybe he can dig up something. You get back to Davidson. Don't lose him."

But when he's alone, The Nose doesn't phone Castellano immediately. Instead, he puts in a call to The Man from Chicago. He reports on the progress of the egg search, how all the bozos are on the street trying to find out who made any recent purchases of liquid nitrogen.

"Very good," The Man says approvingly. "Sounds like you got things organized."

"Yeah," Zucchi says, "but something just came up that maybe you should know about."

Then he tells Chicago how Sam Davidson has been visiting this weirdo on Park Avenue, a richnik named Champ DuBois who drives a white Jag and leaks money.

"I figured I'd call Castellano and ask him to run a trace on the guy."

"No," The Man says sharply, "don't do that. This is our business, and I don't want Rocco to know a thing about it. Got that straight?"

"Oh, sure," The Nose says, swallowing hard and trying to remember exactly how much he's already told Castellano.

"You see, Mario," The Man says in a kindly tone, "technically we're in violation of the rules. I mean, we got from Chicago west, but we got no right to operate in New York. If Rocco hears about it, he'll blow his stack. I'd do the same if he tried to work a deal here or in Vegas or LA. So it'd be better if he's kept in the dark. You cappish?"

"I cappish," Zucchi says miserably. "We'll wrap up this whole megillah as fast as we can and then get out of town—right?"

"Right," The Man says. "We don't want to start a war, do we, Mario?"

As soon as he's off the phone, The Nose pours himself a belt of booze and gulps it down. Then pours another. And another. He wonders how much more of this egg hunt his liver can stand.

Cairo, Egypt

Fearing his hotel room may be bugged, despite daily electronic sweeps, Control assembles his field agents near the Great Pyramid of Khufu at Giza. "They can't bug a desert," Control points out.

The agents, Ptolemy Ramses and Tut, squat in the sand, swelter, and warily eye the cameleers waiting for tourists. It seems to them that Control might have selected a more salubrious spot for a secret meeting, someplace air-conditioned or at least shaded. But Control never sweats.

"All right," he says briskly, "let's get this show on the road. Re the theft of Marilyn Taylor's eggs . . . Langley has assigned it a Red One classification. The action is code-named Operation Soufflé, and we're elected to carry the oblate spheriod until the situation has been either maximized or minimized. Meanwhile, a jump team has been alerted in case it's needed, and units of the Sixth Fleet will be on call. Langley wants all the stops jerked out on this one."

"What if Youssef Khalidi is giving us a lot of kaka," Ptolemy says.

"Then we'll fold our tents like the Arabs and as silently steal away. But until we definitely determine that Joe is bhanged out of his gourd, we'll give Operation Soufflé the highest priority. Here are your assignments. . . .

"Ptolemy, you'll be point man with Khalidi. Try to find out who his informant is and then cut old Joe out of the loop so we can deal directly with the source.

"Ramses, you liaise with the Scones, Croissants, and Bagels. See if they've picked up any gabble about Marilyn's eggs. Play it cool; don't even hint we have a king-size flap on our hands.

"Tut, your job is to find out what you can about Arm of God, the terrorist sect that supposedly grabbed Marilyn's eggs for ransom. Start out by talking to that cross-eyed mullah who sold the embassy the fake Kirman."

"How much can we spend?" Tut asks.

"Up to a thousand dollars Yank. More than that, get my okay first. Any more questions? No? Good. Then let's get cracking on Operation Soufflé. Langley wants daily updates on this one."

That evening, Ptolemy meets with Khalidi at the Coney Island Café. The agent is bemused to note that the water in Youssef's hubble-bubble contains several rose petals and what appears to be a handful of spearmint Tic-Tacs. The CIA man, whose stomach has finally subsided to dull rumblings, orders a bottle of Heineken.

"Joe," he starts earnestly, "about those eggs . . ."

Khalidi presses a grimy forefinger against one nostril, leans over the floor, and violently exhales through the open nostril. He inspects the result. Ptolemy doesn't look.

"Ah, yes, effendi," Youssef says. "The eggs of your movie queen. Sad. Very sad."

"You told me they were stolen by a terrorist organization called Arm of God."

Joe puts that same forefinger in front of his lips.

"Quieter," he says. "The walls have eyes."

"Ears," Ptolemy says.

"What?"

"The walls have ears."

"That is so?" Khalidi says, puzzled. "Then what has eyes?"

The CIA man shrugs. "Potatoes. Storms. Needles. Tell me something: Where did you get your information about Marilyn's eggs?"

"Oh, no," Youssef says. "No, no, no. It would mean my life." He draws the all-purpose forefinger across his throat.

"How much?" Ptolemy asks in a low voice.

"Five hundred American."

"One."

"Four."

"Two."

"Three."

"Two-fifty," the agent says, "and that's my limit."

"Done," Khalidi says. "I learned of this matter from a man named Akmed."

"Akmed *what?* Or *what* Akmed? What's his full name?"

"I know him only as Akmed."

Ptolemy gazes out at the dance floor where an anorexic belly dancer is oscillating to the jazz combo's rendition of "Let a Smile Be Your Umbrella on a Rainy Day." She has a very demure navel, the agent notes. Hardly large enough to accommodate a jumbo California olive, pitted.

"Akmed," he repeats. "I'd like to meet him."

"That would not be wise, effendi," Joe says. "Akmed is a violent man. If he knew I was talking to you, I fear he would seek revenge against me and my grandmother. Beneath his robes he carries a scimitar. Very sharp."

"Where does he live?"

"Here, there, everywhere. He moves frequently."

"That's interesting," Ptolemy says thoughtfully. "You think he belongs to Arm of God?"

"It is possible."

"Has he told you anything else about Marilyn's eggs?"

"Three hundred American."

"All right," the agent says testily. "What did he say?"

"The eggs were taken from Beirut to a safe house in the Bekaa region. Now, Akmed says, it is planned to move them to south Lebanon."

"Near the Israeli border?"

"Yes."

"Why there? Is the PLO in on this?"

Youssef Khalidi gives him a hooded stare. "It is possible, effendi," he says.

Ptolemy repeats this conversation to Control, in the cocktail lounge of the latter's hotel.

"The PLO," the field agent emphasizes. "Marilyn's movies do very well in Tel Aviv. Maybe the PLO is planning a blackmail scheme."

"Uh-huh," Control says, frowning. "I don't like the sound of this. It could be bigger than we thought. We've got to make contact with Akmed."

"I've been thinking about that," Ptolemy says. "Suppose I tail Khalidi? He might lead me to Akmed."

"You think you can handle it? This is a devilish town to get around in. Even the alleys have alleys."

"I can give it a try."

"All right," Control says, "you do that. But watch your back. Or we'll find you floating down the Nile with your schlong in your mouth."

Queens, NY

A choice gaggle of goons wait at the bar in Rocco Castellano's steakhouse. The don and his underboss are in the back room going over lists of names and addresses in the New York area where liquid nitrogen may be purchased.

"Mario Zucchi may be ahead of us on the search," Vito Zivic says, "but not by much."

"What he's doing is illegal," Castellano says somberly. "According to the Treaty of Hackensack, signed in 1986, everyone agreed not to invade another guy's territory. Not for any kind of business. Not even a vacation without tipping off the boss. And now The Man from Chicago sends Zucchi to New York on the qt, hoping to make a big score. It's just not proper. How would he like it if I was to take out a bank in Vegas, say, or hit an armored truck in LA."

"What if Mario finds Marilyn's eggs before we do, Rocco? What happens then?"

"We might have to go to the futons," Castellano says darkly, "I'll talk to the other Families about this, and see if they'll back me up. I tell you, if Mario finds those eggs before we do, the shit will really hit the fan. You ever been in an all-out war?"

"No, I never have."

"Well, it ain't fun. But sometimes you gotta do it to keep the peace. Now let's get those guys on the street. You give them their orders and tell them to use muscle if they have to. All I want is results."

After Zivic leaves, Castellano sits for a few moments drumming blunt fingers on his desk top. Then he picks up the phone and calls The Man from Chicago.

"Hey, *compagno,*" he says cheerily, "how's your health?"

"Couldn't be better, Rocco, thank God. And you?"

"Not a care in the world."

"Glad to hear it. What's on your mind?"

"Listen, I thought I'd take a few days off, fly to Vegas, lose some money. I just wanted you to know that me and Vito Zivic will be going out for some laughs."

"It's right and proper that you should tell me," The Man says approvingly. "Shows respect. You'll be staying at my joint?"

"If it's okay with you."

"I'd be insulted if you didn't. I'll call and tell them to lay it on for you. How long will you be there?"

"Oh, maybe a week or so. I gotta get out of New York and breathe some fresh air."

"Good idea. Stay as long as you like. You're comped; you know that. It's good you should take some time off. Recharge your batteries."

"That's what I figure on doing. My organization can get along without me for a week; it's not going to fall apart."

"You're doing the right thing, Rocco."

Castellano hangs up. *"Bastardo!"* he says aloud, satisfied he's got Chicago thinking that he'll be leaving town and Mario Zucchi will be free to find Marilyn's eggs without competition.

Then Castellano calls the dons of the other local Families. If they're not in, he talks to their consiglieres. He sets up a meet at his home in Forest Hills. If push comes to shove, he wants New York to present a united front against Chicago.

It's not so much the million dollars; it's the principle of the thing.

Manhattan, NY

"Nice of you to stop by," Marilyn Taylor says bitterly. "You want an autographed photo—right?"

Detective McBryde, who has spent a frustrating day hitting the five Yum-Yum Burger Shoppes in Queens without results, is in no mood to take any shit from this prima donna.

"The investigation is proceeding," he says stiffly. "If I have to report to you every hour on the hour, it'll take twice as long. Is that what you want?"

"All I want is my eggs."

"You'll get them."

"You swear to that?" she demands.

"No, I won't swear to that. I won't even swear that the sun will rise tomorrow. But the chances are good that the eggs will be recovered."

"Nobody gives a good goddamn about my eggs," she says wrathfully. "A couple of weeks from now all the ballyhoo will die down, and my poor little eggs will be lost forever."

He stares at her. "I knew you had a lot of faults, but I didn't think self-pity was one of them. Stop feeling so sorry for yourself. Believe me, a lot of women have suffered worse tragedies in their lives."

"So the theft of my eggs is just chopped liver to you—right?"

"I didn't say that. A crime has been committed, and the Department is doing everything it can to solve it. But if you don't get your eggs back, it won't be the end of the world."

"That's easy for you to say. You're just a lousy *man.*"

He sighs and rises. "May I go home now? I've had a rough day, and I'm hungry."

Suddenly she is all soft sympathy. "You mean you haven't had any dinner?"

"That's what I mean."

"Why the hell didn't you say so. Come on downstairs and let's see what's available."

In the kitchen she sits him down at the white enamel work table and sets a place for him. From the big refrigerator she drags half a barbecued chicken, a small baked ham, a pot of beans, a bowl of salad, a key lime pie, a bottle of Molson's ale. She puts it all out in front of him.

"Go ahead," she says, "feed your face."

"Nothing for you?"

"I ate hours ago. Maybe I'll have a slice of pie to keep you company. I made it myself."

"You're kidding?"

"That's right, I'm kidding. But I can cook. I'm not totally plastic, you know."

He leans over his food. "I know," he says in a low voice.

He scoffs chicken, ham, beans, salad, ale. Then he pushes back from the table. "Good grub," he says. "Thank you."

"A wedge of pie?"

"No, thanks. I never eat desserts."

She honks a laugh. "How about me?" she asks.

Up in that frilly bedroom, he insists on first taking a shower.

"I smell like a goat," he explains.

"Sometimes that can be fun," she says, and he shakes his head at such depravity.

Ten minutes later, when he comes out of the bathroom, he finds her naked, sprawled lazily on the silken sheet, mauve this time.

"I used your perfumed soap," he announces.

"You're entitled," she says, reaching for him. "McBryde, you ever been around the world?"

"No," he says seriously, "but I've been to Europe twice."

She giggles at such innocence. "Come to momma," she says, "and I'll take you on a trip."

It takes them more than an hour to complete their journey. Then, surfeited, they look at each other with wondering eyes.

"Whatever happens with my eggs," she says, "whether you find them or you don't, eventually I'll be going back to the Coast. And that'll be that. You understand?"

He nods.

"As long as you know," she goes on. "I'm not ready for any long-term commitments."

"You don't have to draw a diagram," he says.

"You don't want a heavy involvement either, do you?"

"No," he says.

"Then we can have a few giggles together, and no one gets hurt."

"Sounds good to me."

"There's just one thing I ask."

"What's that?"

"Cut your goddamned toenails. I'm all scratched up."

"Listen," he says, "I better be getting home."

"Not yet," she says. "Let's cuddle awhile."

Manhattan, NY

Sam Davidson is beginning to wonder if reincarnationists haven't stumbled upon a great truth. The possibility that thousands of years ago his soul inhabited the body of a scurvy knave who committed Heinous Sins is the only explanation he can think of why now, in his present embodiment, he is suffering such an outrageous fate; it is punishment for his transgressions in a previous existence.

Never, in his most frightful nightmares, did he ever dream that one day he would be an indentured servant to a professional thief. And forced by that minatorial lunatic to tramp the streets of Manhattan, looking for someone who sold liquid nitrogen to someone who swiped Marilyn Taylor's eggs. As a producer of porn films, Sam is inured to working with implausible scripts. But this, the scenario of his own life, he'd give the old heave-ho. Just too wacko.

His first intention was to accept the list graciously from Champ, vow he would give the search his best shot, and then spend the day in the skin-flick palaces on Eighth Avenue, checking out the competition. He would eventually return to the Park Avenue apartment and report failure. But he was out-hustled.

"You can depend on my complete cooperation," he tells the goofball.

"I know I can," DuBois says with his sharklike grin. "One of Mutha's lads may double-check the places you visit just to make sure."

"Oh," Sam says.

So here he is with a list of liquid nitrogen sources from 14th Street south to the Battery. He is to use the same con all of Mutha's crew have been taught: They are reporters from a weekly tabloid called *The National Rocket.* They are working on a story about the theft of Marilyn's eggs. They have even been supplied with fake ID.

Surprisingly, the first two suppliers Davidson hits are willing to cooperate. But the only nitrogen they've sold recently has been to hospitals and clinics. The next three refuse to give him the time of day.

Davidson slogs on down to Canal Street, feet beginning to ache from this unaccustomed pounding on city pavements. And behind him, just as footsore, plods Dino, the bentnose assigned by Mario Zucchi to shadow Sam. Dino is praying to God that his target will stop for a beer and a pizza.

The joint on Canal Street is something else again. It's an old attic of a place that sells new and used laboratory, surgical, and medical equipment and supplies. It's a hodgepodge of wheelchairs, hospital beds, walkers, canes, crutches, and a lot of stainless steel gadgets that Davidson can't identify. There's a patina of dust on everything, and jolly hand-lettered signs: "Get your vacation bandages *now!*" and "Ask for our holiday special on enema bags."

The whole place seems to be operated by one guy, a tub of lard wearing camouflage jeans and a T-shirt that says, "A douche a day keeps the doctor away." His doughy face sags in melancholy folds. Which is understandable, Sam figures, if you spend all your working hours amid secondhand bedpans.

"Help you?" the guy asks in a raspy basso profundo.

"Are you the owner?"

"That's me. Thornton G. Kalbacker. What can I do you for?"

"You sell liquid nitrogen?"

"How much you want?"

"I don't want to buy any," Davidson says, and then launches into his scam: He's a reporter working for *The National Rocket* on a story about the theft of Marilyn Taylor's eggs. All he'd like to know is whether or not any liquid nitrogen has been sold recently.

Kalbacker stares at him. "You think the crooks need liquid nitrogen to keep the eggs frozen, so you're checking up on anyone who bought the stuff. Am I right?"

"You're a smart man, Mr. Kalbacker, and you're exactly right. Have you made any recent sales?"

The owner gives him a wisenheimer grin. "What's in it for me?" he asks.

"You'll get your name in *The National Rocket.*"

"That won't buy any kasha knishes."

Champ DuBois has authorized his egg hunters to pay fifty dollars, if necessary, to obtain information. Davidson reckons he can chisel some of that.

"I am authorized to pay twenty dollars, tops, for any valuable leads you can provide."

"Twenty? You'll have to do better than that."

"If I pay you more," Sam says piteously, "it comes out of my own pocket."

"I don't care where it comes from; I want fifty."

"Fifty?" Davidson cries, anguished. "No way. Forty is the best I can do."

"All right," the fat man says, "I'll go easy on you; forty it is. Let's see the color of your money."

Sam takes out his wallet, then pauses. "What if you stiff me?" he says. "I pay, and then you tell me no one bought any liquid nitrogen from you. That ain't worth forty bucks."

Kalbacker shrugs. "You don't trust me?" he asks. "Okay, the deal is dead. It's your decision."

Sam groans and hands over two twenty-dollar bills. "You're a sharp man, Mr. Kalbacker."

"No sharper than you. Your boss probably told you to pay fifty for a hot tip, and you're figuring to pocket the other ten. Am I right?"

"Enough of this high finance," Davidson says. "What's your hot tip?"

"A couple of days ago a guy comes in. I never seen him before or since. At first I thought he was a young kid. But up close, I see he's maybe thirty years old. Around there. A blondie. Hair high in front and slicked down in back. He's wearing a black leather jacket, and I thought he might be a biker who came in to rip me off. I been taken four times this year, so far. But no, all he wanted was to buy some liquid nitrogen."

"Did he say what for?"

"I ast him that. He claimed he was buying it for a foot doctor on Staten Island. I thought that was a crock because you can buy the stuff on Staten Island. But he showed me the doctor's business card, so I sold him three liters of the soup in a refrigerator jug. What the hell, a sale's a sale. Am I right?"

"How did he pay for it?"

"Cash."

"Did you ask for his address?"

"What would I want to do that for? Listen, I could tell he wasn't going to become a regular customer. I just made sure he knew how to handle it okay. Liquid nitrogen is harmless if it's treated right. But if the container isn't vented, it can become a bomb. He said he'd make sure the vents in the lid were kept clean and open. Then he picked up his jug and left."

"A blond guy in a black leather jacket? That's all you can tell me?"

"Wearing a white T-shirt and jeans. That's about it."

"Shit," Sam says disgustedly. "There must be a million guys like that in New York."

"Probably."

"We'll never find him."

"Maybe you can. Give me that other tenner, and I'll tell you how."

Davidson is outraged. "You're a real gonif," he says angrily.

"It takes one to know one. Do I get the ten?"

Sam hands it over. "Well?"

"I told you he showed me the business card of a podiatrist. I don't recall the doctor's name, but I remember the town where he has his office because it's the same as my first name: Thornton. There's your hot tip. How many foot doctors can there be in Thornton, Staten Island? Am I right?"

Manhattan, NY

"Mario, I *couldna* called you before," Dino says, much aggrieved. "The guy goes into this dump on Canal Street and then comes running like a bat outta hell. He grabs a cab. You told me to tail him, dinya? By the time I get a cab, he's outta sight. But I figure the odds are two to one he's heading for the apartment on Park. So I come up here and sure enough, my pal, the doorman, he tells me Davidson showed up a few minutes ago and went up to see that Champ DuBois. I'm calling from a phone in the lobby which I had to slip the doorman a fin so I could use it."

"All right, all right," Zucchi says impatiently, "I get the picture. You stay there in case Davidson comes out. Then you stick to him."

"I done good, din I, Mario?"

"Yeah," The Nose says sourly, "you done good."

He hangs up and considers the implications of what Dino has told him. It's obvious to Zucchi that Davidson has been hitting sources of liquid nitrogen in lower Manhattan, and struck it rich on Canal Street. Then he hustled back to Champ DuBois to tell him the good news.

Mario glances at his Cartier rip-off. Too late to find out what Davidson discovered. But Zucchi vows to be at that Canal Street joint first thing tomorrow morning.

Everyone knows it ain't over until it's over.

Staten Island, NY

Early in the morning, Champ DuBois and Mutha slide into the white Jaguar and start their trip to the terra incognita of Staten Island. Since neither of them has often been south of Manhattan's 23rd Street, they have prepared for this perilous journey by bringing along a quart thermos of vodka gimlets and two small crystal goblets.

They are fascinated by the ferry ride and awed by the marine activity in the Upper Bay. Arriving safely at Staten Island, they inquire of a deckhand the best route to Thornton. Champ casually offers a sawbuck, and they are given explicit instructions.

"Don't drive too fast," the roustabout counsels, patting the fender of the Jag, "or you'll pass it before you see it. It's just a shopping mall with a few houses around."

That's exactly what Thornton turns out to be, and after consulting the local telephone directory and asking a genial peeler guarding the parking lot, they discover that the only podiatrist for miles around is Dr. Leopold Gingle, with an office in the mall.

Dr. Gingle's receptionist is a tall, willowy black lady who looks somewhat askance at Champ DuBois' costume: dark specs, white linen jumpsuit, wide-brimmed planter's sombrero with a snakeskin band.

"May I help you?" she asks, pleasantly enough.

"Indeed you may, sister," Champ says. "We have urgent business with the good doctor."

"Could you tell me what it's about? The doctor is busy with a patient right now."

"Well, don't you disturb him, sister," DuBois says, giving her a flash of his California whites. "I'll do that. Mutha, suppose you stay here and entertain the sister."

"I'm no sister of yours," she yells after him as he goes barging into the inner office.

Dr. Gingle is seated before a robust matron, applying plaster to bandages wrapped about her left foot and ankle. The doctor is a smallish man with a wispy mustache, a high balding brow, and a low boiling point. He looks up wrathfully at DuBois.

"What is the meaning of this intrusion?" he demands.

"Love the way you talk," Champ says. "Just *love* it. I apologize for my unconventional behavior, doc—and you too, ma'am. But I need some information I hope and trust you can provide."

"Remove yourself from these premises immediately," Dr. Gingle says sternly, "or I shall be forced to summon the police."

"What a mouth on you," DuBois marvels. "It goes like a whippoorwill's ass." He slides a long pearl-handled knife from the pocket of his jumpsuit and presses a button. A shiny steel blade flicks into position and locks. "This snickersnee is for effect," he explains. "Just to impress you."

The patient is looking at him with mouth agape. "You want drugs," she bursts out. "You're going to steal drugs."

"Oh, no, ma'am," Champ says, "I don't indulge. Just a little information and then I'll be on my way. Doc, you use liquid nitrogen in your tootsy work?"

"Occasionally," Dr. Gingle says cautiously.

"Uh-huh. Now here's the sixty-four-dollar question. Think carefully about this one. You ever have a patient like this: a young-looking blond guy. Wears his hair high in front, slicked down in back. He's like thirty years old. White T-shirt, jeans, black leather jacket. You ever have a patient like that?"

"The doctor-patient relationship is privileged," the podiatrist says frostily. "I can't reveal that information."

DuBois takes one quick step and holds the point of his steel blade almost inside Gingle's right nostril.

"You'd look funny without a honker, my man," he says gently. "Think hard about that young blond guy."

"Maybe," the doctor says hoarsely, his eyes almost crossed as he focuses on the knife point. "About a year ago. Plantar wart. It responded to liquid nitrogen."

"Sounds good to me," Champ says. "Name and address, please. The sooner you dig them up, the sooner I'm long gone."

The doctor fumbles a card from his desk file with trembling fingers. DuBois plucks the card away and slides it into his pocket.

"Many thanks for your kind cooperation, doc," he says. "Listen, I think I'm getting a callus on the ball of my right foot. Can you suggest anything?"

"Not without an examination."

"Maybe some other time," Champ says, folding up his knife. "One more thing: Please don't inform the authorities of my visit. I don't think that would be wise a'tall. Now you just go on with your treatment. I hope your foot will be feeling better, ma'am," he adds politely.

Then he's out the door, collects Mutha, and flips a hand at the comely receptionist.

"See you around, sister," he calls.

"Not if I see you first," she says hotly.

In the Jaguar, he reads the card taken from Dr. Gingle's file. "Ronald Yates. Mutha, ask that nice gendarme how we find West New Brighton."

But they get lost twice, and it's late afternoon before they pull up in front of the Yates's bungalow.

"A palace," Champ says, eyeballing the house. "Reminds me of my forefathers' mansion in deepest Alabam'."

He opens the glove compartment and pokes about in the jumble. He comes up with an ornate badge, silver and gold, very impressive. But close examination would reveal the legend: GARTER INSPECTOR.

"Let's go," he says to Mutha. "You got your shooter?"

"Yeth, mutha," Mutha says.

DuBois raps on the warped frame of the screen door. After a few moments, the inner door is opened by a blond guy in jeans and a white T-shirt.

"Yeah?" he says.

"Mr. Ronald Yates?" Champ asks.

"That's right. Who are you?"

DuBois flashes his badge swiftly. "New York City Public Services Department," he says. "Bureau of Water, Electricity, Gas, and Television. We have a report of a gas leak in the neighborhood, and we're checking every house. Could we come in for a moment, please."

"I don't smell anything," Ronnie says.

"Just take a minute," Champ says patiently. "It's for your own safety, sir. Wouldn't want to be launched sky-high, would you?"

Yates lets them in. They glance into the living room where Mrs. Gertrude Yates has her eyes glued on the TV set. Then they go into the kitchen, and DuBois sniffs suspiciously.

"Perhaps," he says. "Perhaps not. Let's go upstairs."

"There are no gas appliances up there," Ronald says.

"But escaping gas rises, y'see. Oh, yes. Collects on the top floor. That's where we'll be able to tell if you've got a leak."

So they troop up to the second floor, where DuBois and Mutha search every room and closet. Then Champ turns the knob of a locked door.

"What's in here?" he asks.

"Nothing. A storeroom."

"Unlock the door, please."

"It's just a lot of junk," Ronnie protests.

"Open the door, or we shall be forced to call an officer of the law."

Yates unlocks the door. DuBois swings it wide and stands on the threshold. He stares at Marilyn Taylor posters on the walls, Marilyn Taylor photographs, Marilyn Taylor magazine covers, newspaper clippings, a framed portrait, video cassettes.

"Oh my," he says softly.

He steps into the shrine and sees the two white containers, one small, one large.

"What's in those?" he asks.

"Lemonade," Ronnie says manfully.

DuBois stoops, removes the lid of the larger jug, holds his palm over the mouth.

"Liquid nitrogen," he proclaims. He straightens, looks at Yates accusingly. "Sir," he says, "do you have an official permit to store volatile liquids in a closed space in a domestic establishment?"

Ronald hangs his head. "No," he says in a low voice, "but it's just a little bit."

"A potential bomb," DuBois cries. "Blow up the whole fucking neighborhood. Sir, we'll have to confiscate these containers and hold them in a protected area of headquarters until you obtain the required permit."

"Please," Yates says, raising his head, "don't take them. They're mine. They're very valuable to me."

"Regulations must be followed," Champ says severely. "Everyone knows that. Inspector, take these to the car immediately."

His majordomo picks up both refrigerator jugs with no apparent effort and leaves. DuBois remains with Yates until Mutha is down the stairs and out of the house.

Ronnie is bewildered. "How do I get them back?" he asks in a shaken voice.

"File a formal application with the General Services Administration."

"I thought you said you're from the Public Services Department."

"Same thing," DuBois says, and takes a final look around the shrine. "I do admire your taste, sir. She is a total woman."

Yates follows him downstairs, watches him help the other man store the containers in the back of the white Jaguar. It is only then that Ronnie realizes the enormity of his loss, and tears come to his eyes. He runs shakily toward the Jag, but it pulls away quickly and he watches it recede in the distance.

He is still standing there, weeping quietly, when a dusty blue Plymouth pulls up and parks in front of his home. A tall, rangy man wearing a black three-piece suit gets out and strides up to him.

"Mr. Ronald Yates?" he asks.

Staten Island, NY

Detective Lieutenant Jeffrey McBryde spends most of the morning explaining to Deputy Inspector Gripsholm why he's devoting so much time searching for a blond guy in a black leather jacket who has a Yum-Yum Burger Shoppe decal in the back window of his antique Volkswagen. When he finishes his recital, Gripsholm stares at him.

"It's *Looney Tunes* time, folks," he says.

"Sure it is," McBryde says equably. "Want me to drop it?"

"Jesus, no! We're still getting static on this. Everyone from the White House on down. We've even had inquiries from the CIA, plus daily calls from the FBI wanting to know what we know. Which, at the moment, is zilch."

"I wouldn't say that—exactly."

"You really think this Yum-Yum decal lead will pan out?"

The lieutenant shrugs. "It's all we've got."

"All right then," Gripsholm says, "stick with it for a while. If you find blondie and the eggs, send me a rocket."

So the detective requisitions a blue Plymouth that was ready for a trade-in five years ago. He gets over to Staten Island in the afternoon and starts with the Yum-Yum Burger Shoppe in West New Brighton. He goes through the same drill he used in Brooklyn and Queens: finds the manager, flashes his tin, asks if any of the employees is a blond guy, maybe in his early thirties, who drives a beat-up Volkswagen with a Yum-Yum decal on the back window.

He's prepared for another defeat, but the manager says anxiously, "He's not in any trouble, is he?"

McBryde's hopes leap like a startled hart. "Nah," he says, "no trouble. But he may have witnessed a car accident, and I need some information. What's his name?"

"Ronald Yates. We call him Ronnie."

"Is he working now?"

"Comes on at six tonight," the manager says. "A fantastic burger flipper. Can do two at a time, a spatula in each hand."

"That's really interesting," Lieutenant McBryde says. "Could I have his home address, please."

When he gets to Yates's place, there's a young-looking blond guy standing out on the scrabbly lawn. The detective marches up to him and says, "Mr. Ronald Yates?"

The fellow turns, nods, and McBryde can see that he's been crying. So he hits him hard while he's vulnerable: "Where are Marilyn's eggs?" he demands.

"They took them," Yates says.

"Who took them?"

"The gas inspectors."

"What gas inspectors?"

"The ones in the white Jaguar."

The lieutenant looks up at the sky. He feels like weeping himself. But he displays his shield and ID. "Lieutenant Jeffrey McBryde, NYPD. Ronnie, let's go inside and talk awhile—okay?"

The shrine has already been violated by strangers, so Ronald takes him up there. McBryde gapes at the decorations, then looks at the lad with sympathy. He wonders how long it'll be before *he* tacks a Marilyn Taylor poster over his bed.

"Let's start at the beginning," he says. "How did you know about Nicholas Kazanian?"

"Who?"

"Kazanian. The guy you stole the eggs from."

"I never knew his name."

Then Yates explains how he was outside the fertility clinic on East 70th Street on the Saturday night it was robbed. One of the crooks gave him a book of matches, and after he heard of the theft on the news, he decided to go to Turk's Bar in Brooklyn and get her eggs back.

"I even bought some liquid nitrogen," he says earnestly, "so I could keep them fresh."

"Why didn't you return them to Marilyn?" the detective asks gently.

"I don't know," Ronnie mumbles. "They were like, you know, a souvenir."

"Uh-huh," McBryde says, guessing there's more to it than that. "So now you've got the flask of eggs and a container of liquid nitrogen. How do the gas inspectors come into this?"

Yates says they got into the house by claiming there was a gas leak in the neighborhood and they had to check every home.

"Did they show you any identification?"

Well, the tall black flashed a badge, but Ronnie didn't see what was on it. He said he was from the Public Services Department—or something like that.

"If they were looking for a gas leak, why did they take the eggs?"

"Because they said it was against the law to store volatile liquids in a residence."

"You didn't think it strange that New York City gas inspectors would be driving a Jaguar?"

Uh, Ronald didn't actually see the car until it was too late. They just loaded up the Jag and drove away.

"Beautiful," McBryde says. "Can you describe the two men?"

One was this skinny black wearing a white jumpsuit, dark sunglasses, and a wide-brimmed straw sombrero with a snakeskin band. The other man was short, very old, looked like an Oriental of some kind, and he was wearing a black silk pajama suit with a dragon embroidered on the back of the jacket.

"Typical gas inspectors," the lieutenant nods solemnly. "No wonder you were fooled. Was the Jaguar a two-door or four?"

"Two."

"Did you see the license plate?"

"Just for a few seconds."

"Remember it? Or any part of it?"

"I think it had the numbers eight and six and one in it, but I don't remember in what order."

"All right. I want to talk to you more about this, Ronnie, but right now I've got to use your phone."

"There's one in my bedroom."

"Come in with me, please."

McBryde calls Sergeant Rumfry. "This is hot," he says rapidly. "Start a vehicle search for a white two-door Jaguar, model unknown, possibly leaving Staten Island for Manhattan in the next hour. Get down to the ferry terminal. You're looking for two guys. One tall, skinny black, one short Oriental. Both dressed like they're going to a masquerade party. If you nab them, sit on them until I get there."

"What's the charge?"

"They've got Marilyn's eggs."

"No shit? I'll get right on it."

McBryde and Yates go back into the shrine. The lieutenant examines the library of Marilyn's video cassettes, and wonders if he should get a VCR.

"Ronnie," he says, "eventually you'll have to come over to Manhattan, dictate a formal statement, and sign it. But right now I'd like to go over your story again to make sure I've got it straight."

"You're not going to arrest me, are you?" Ronald says nervously.

The detective smiles sadly. "What for? Unrequited love in the first degree?"

Boston, MA

The two old geezers are at it again. They settle comfortably into their leather club chairs, sip their brandies appreciatively, puff gently on their good cigars, and wonder what more life could possibly offer to top their present content.

"I had a visitor today," says Professor T. Hiram Farthingale. "That very intense young man from the Federal Bureau of Investigation."

"Ah-ha," says Monsignor Terence Evelyn O'Dell. "Getting antsy, are they?"

"Oh, yes," the professor says, permitting himself a dry chuckle. "They are most anxious that I declare the theft of Marilyn's eggs a kidnapping. But I explained I cannot do that until my legal research has been completed."

O'Dell smiles. "I am honored that you consider our debates to be legal research. Do you think you will ever render a final opinion?"

"I may. I may not. I don't believe it is of any great import since the crime is being investigated by the New York Police Department."

"With apparently no results, if the newspaper and television reports are to be believed. Perhaps the eggs will never be recovered, and their theft will remain an unsolved mystery. Like the disappearance of Judge Crater or what actually happened at Fall River."

"Help yourself to the cognac. I'm too cozy to move."

"And a little more for you?"

"If you would, please."

"Terry, why do you suppose the theft of Marilyn's eggs has generated worldwide interest and continues to receive exhaustive coverage by the media?"

The monsignor stirs restlessly, fearing a legalistic trap. "I should think the reasons are obvious. It is a unique and outré crime. And the victim is a movie star of the first magnitude who has justly been named The Most Beautiful Woman in the World."

"Mmm. I wonder if that is not too facile an explanation. Let me suggest to you that the general concern is not so much engendered by the victim as it is by the swag."

"The eggs?"

"Precisely."

"Hiram, if you intend to provoke my curiosity, you are succeeding admirably. Why should the eggs be an object of universal perturbation?"

"Consider the egg. Human or chicken, it makes no difference. But since man first walked upright upon the earth, the egg has occupied a special niche in his consciousness. It has been a symbol of regeneration. It has almost mythic properties."

"Ho-ho! So you agree with me as to the potentiality of the egg."

"What I suggest to you is that the egg stirs something primitive in all of us. Our veneration of the egg predates and transcends organized religion and organized law. It goes back to a people wearing animal pelts and huddling around a fire in a cave. This worship of the egg antedates your church and my law. We all carry vestigial remains of that ancient belief. We have a racial memory of the holiness of eggs. And the news that one woman's eggs have been stolen and perhaps destroyed arouses that antediluvian instinct, and we are shocked and outraged that a beloved icon should be so despoiled."

Monsignor O'Dell is silent a long moment, then sighs mightily. "An original and imaginative concept, Hiram, but how does your encomium on the egg relate to the matter at hand: was the theft of Marilyn's eggs a kidnapping or was it not?"

Farthingale pauses before answering. Then: "It has caused me to question if the theft might not be classified as a crime against humanity since it strikes at one of our most elemental and cherished spiritual beliefs."

"A crime against humanity," O'Dell repeats. "Would that come under the jurisdiction of the Federal Bureau of Investigation?"

"I would have to research the matter," the professor says, "but I doubt it. If the theft of Marilyn's eggs can be established as a crime against humanity, then I should think the proper agency to investigate the grave offense would be the United Nations."

The monsignor nods thoughtfully. "Shall we have more brandy?" he suggests. "And perhaps another cigar."

Manhattan, NY

In his ragtag emporium on Canal Street, Thornton G. Kalbacker is using a feather duster on an attractive display of new and used trusses and wondering if he should mark down a job lot of wooden pessaries purchased from a bankrupt Guatemalan.

The street door bangs open, and two heavies stalk in. Kalbacker makes them for a couple of wallyos, hard guys wearing California threads. The bigger of the two looks like he was hacked from Mount Rushmore. The leader is not much smaller and has a schnozzle that doesn't end.

"Yes, sir, gentlemen," the merchant says affably, "what can I do you for?"

"You got liquid nitrogen?" The Nose demands.

"Of course. I got everything. How much you want?"

"I don't want to buy any," Mario Zucchi says. "I just want to know who bought some in the last week or so."

"Oh, I can't remember that. I have so many customers, I can't keep track."

"Yeah," Zucchi says, looking around the grimy, deserted store, "I'll bet you're busy as hell. You the owner?"

"That's right. Thornton G. Kalbacker, at your service."

"Well, Mr. Kalbacker, stop waltzing me around. A fatso came in here yesterday afternoon, asked you the same question I just asked, and you told him. Am I right?"

"Could be. But of course he properly reimbursed me for my cooperation."

Zucchi sighs and pulls out his wallet. "You New York k'nackers are all alike. How much did he pay you?"

"A hundred."

"Bull*shit!*" Mario says. "If he sprang for fifty, I'd be surprised. That's what I'll pay."

"It's gotta be a hundred," Kalbacker repeats stubbornly.

"It don't gotta be *anything*," The Nose says. He motions toward the mastodon. "Sally, show him."

Sally looks around a moment, then selects an adjustable stainless steel cane and, with no apparent effort, twists it into a neat bowknot.

"Okay, fifty bucks," the owner says hastily. "Plus twenty for the cane," he adds.

Zucchi pays him, and Kalbacker relates the same story he told Sam Davidson the previous afternoon.

The Nose glances at his counterfeit Cartier. "Shit," he says disgustedly, "they must be there by now. Well, there's more than one way to skin a cat."

"I've got some excellent scalpels on sale," the owner says, wanting to be helpful. "Hardly used."

"Some other time. Come on, Sally, let's go back to the Bedlington. Maybe Dino called in."

Kalbacker watches them lumber from his store and slam the street door. He counts the seventy plasters he just earned. He figures he's making more money selling information than peddling embroidered jock straps. Those things just *never* moved.

Manhattan, NY

During his successful career as a thief, Champ DuBois has formulated several axioms that have served to keep him out of the hands of the fuzz. One is that during the commission of a caper, the retreat from the scene of the crime should *always* be by a route different from the approach.

So when he and Mutha have Marilyn's eggs and the container of extra liquid nitrogen safely stowed in the white Jaguar, DuBois seeks another way back to Manhattan rather than taking the ferry. After inquiring at a gas station, they head for the Verrazano Bridge. That takes them to Brooklyn, and eventually to Manhattan via the Williamsburg Bridge.

Traffic is heavy, and it is a long, wearisome trip. But they have the thermos of vodka gimlets to lighten their mood. And they are buoyed by the knowledge that they have accomplished what they set out to do.

"Nothing is more gratifying than a difficult job well done," DuBois remarks sententiously. "I believe we are to be congratulated, Mutha. Don't you?"

"Yeth," Mutha says.

It is late in the evening when they arrive at the Park Avenue apartment house. The doorman breaks off a conversation he's having with a short, burly man and hurries forward to open the door of the Jag. Then he helps carry the two containers into the lobby.

"Feels like cold stuff, Mr. DuBois," he says.

"On the contrary," Champ says, smiling. "It's hot stuff. Thank you for your help, Johann; we can manage from here. Please garage the car; I won't be needing it tonight." He hands over a double-sawbuck.

"Thank *you*, sir. Have a nice evening."

"I intend to," DuBois says, and follows Mutha into the elevator.

Upstairs, they find Sam Davidson rolling on the living room carpet with the Chin twins. All three are giggling, drinking asti spumante from the bottle, and are more than somewhat fuddled. It appears likely, from their flushed faces and disheveled clothing, that they may very well have enjoyed a recent slap-and-tickle.

DuBois orders the young ladies into a back bedroom to prepare for their nightly promenade. Mutha goes behind the bar to mix a fresh batch of vodka gimlets. Meanwhile, Sam Davidson has pulled himself to his feet and is standing shakily, staring at the two white jugs with awe.

"I'll be screwed, blewed, and tattooed," he says. "You did it!"

"Of course we did it," Champ says negligently. He sprawls into his favorite chair and tips his sombrero onto the back of his head. "The result of careful planning, determination, and a healthy dollop of chutzpah. Marilyn's eggs are now ours, along with sufficient liquid nitrogen to keep them in a condition to be ransomed."

"Nice going," Davidson says faintly, fearing what is to come.

"The first act of our creative scenario has been completed," DuBois says, turning his black shades on Sam. "Now you will contact Marilyn to conclude arrangements for what is vulgarly called the payoff."

"Listen," Davidson says hoarsely, "you really think I'm the right guy to handle this?"

"Yes," Champ says coldly, "I really do. Now listen carefully, and I'll tell you exactly how to play your role. Mutha, might we have a bite to eat while we talk?"

"What you like?" Mutha asks.

"Oh, something exotic to celebrate our triumph. What do you suggest?"

"Caviar sandwich on Wonder Bread," Mutha suggests.

"Sounds good to me," DuBois says. "Sam?"

"I'm game," Davidson says despairingly.

Manhattan, NY

Mario Zucchi is somewhat sozzled when Dino finally calls, late in the evening.

"Where the hell you been?" Mario screams at him.

"You think I been living the life of Riley?" Dino says aggrievedly. "Standing around like a mooch on the make. It's a wonder I wasn't collared for loitering. I ain't had a single bite to eat all day."

"All right, all right," The Nose says testily. "What's happening?"

Dino tells him that DuBois has returned to his apartment lugging two white containers.

"Like thermos jugs with handles," Dino says. "One big, one little."

"That blows it," Zucchi says. "They've got Marilyn's eggs. I might as well call off the search. Okay, Dino, quit for the night and get yourself some food. I'll take it from here."

Mario hangs up and stares balefully at the phone. But then he figures he's not in *deep* shit; at least he knows the whereabouts of Marilyn's eggs, and that's a plus. He calls The Man from Chicago and tells him the whole story.

"So now I got the eggs located," he finishes triumphantly.

"I get the picture," The Man says slowly. "Davidson is in bed with this Champ DuBois, and the two of them are going to shake down the Taylor woman. Is that how you see it?"

"That's about it. So what do you want me to do now—crash the apartment and grab the stuff?"

There is silence. It lasts so long that Zucchi finally asks, "You there?"

"I'm here," Chicago says. "I been thinking maybe this is a job for Shakespeare."

"Hey, wait a minute," Zucchi says angrily, emboldened by the booze, "I can handle it. I got enough grunts with me to take the Statue of Liberty. We'll bust into that apartment, snatch the eggs, and take off. If anyone tries to stop us, we'll blow 'em away."

"Mario, Mario," The Man says, sighing, "you still don't cappish. If there's a shoot-'em-up, it'll get in all the papers and on TV. Then Rocco will know we're doing business in his territory. You don't want a war—do you?"

"Guess not."

"Of course not. So we'll do like I say. I'll send Shakespeare to you tomorrow. You show him where the apartment is and let him take it from there."

"I'll do it," The Nose says, "but it's like you don't trust me."

"Just follow my orders, and I'll trust you. Okay?"

"If that's the way it's gotta be."

"That's the way," The Man from Chicago says, and hangs up.

Cairo, Egypt

The belly dancer has a navel as wide as a clown's mouth, and Ptolemy can't take his eyes off her. Until he realizes that with her distracted air and fluttery gestures, she reminds him of his mother. Then, vaguely uneasy, he turns his attention back to Youssef Khalidi, who is drinking arrack and devouring a luncheon of stewed goat with raisin sauce.

"Listen, Joe," the CIA agent says, trying not to inhale the odor of goat, "we've checked with the British, the French, and Israelis. No one's heard of the Arm of God. You sure it exists?"

"It exists, effendi," Khalidi says, wiping his greasy mouth on the sleeve of his burnoose. "Let me prove it." He digs beneath his robe and pulls out a small brass ankh, crudely made and tarnished. "The badge of the Arm of God. Every member carries one for identification."

"How did you get it? Are you a member?"

"No, I bought it at Woolworth's."

"I don't understand. If anyone can buy one, how can the Arm of God gang use it for identification?"

"The real badges are stamped with their enrollment number. For instance, Akmed's ankh is number 513."

"My God, does that mean this terrorist bunch has more than five hundred members?"

"It is possible," Khalidi says. He finishes his lunch and fills his glass again.

"What have you heard recently from Akmed?" Ptolemy asks. "Where are Marilyn's eggs now?"

Youssef looks at him sorrowfully, so the agent digs bills from his wallet and passes them under the table. The other man thumbs them swiftly.

"Only two hundred American?" he whines. "Effendi, I am risking my life and the safety of my grandmother."

"You haven't told me anything useful," Ptolemy points out. "No say, no pay."

Khalidi leans close and lowers his voice. "I can say this: Akmed has just returned from southern Lebanon. The eggs are now being held in a cave very close to the Israeli border."

"A cave? Where is it? Can you pinpoint the exact location?"

"Akmed will not tell. It is high secret."

"Top secret," the agent says.

"What is?"

"What Akmed knows and won't tell. It is called top secret, not high secret."

"Are you certain of this, effendi?"

"Yes, I am certain," Ptolemy says crossly.

There is a new belly dancer on the floor, cavorting to the rhythm of "In the Shade of the Old Apple Tree," played by the jazz combo. Her torso is covered with a loose gauze veil, but from what little the agent can glimpse, her navel appears to be an outsy, shaped somewhat like a golf tee.

"When are you seeing Akmed again?" he asks Khalidi.

"Perhaps this afternoon. Perhaps not."

"Do you think he can be turned?"

"Turned?"

"Get him to work for us. He would continue to belong to the Arm of God, but he would be ours. You understand?"

"I understand, but I do not believe it would be possible. Akmed has much faith in the cause."

"Does he have any weaknesses? Liquor? Drugs? Women?"

"Akmed likes fat boys."

"Fat boys?"

Khalidi nods. *"Clean* fat boys."

"How does he get them?"

"Effendi!" Joe says with a vulpine grin. "He buys them."

"Then he needs money?"

"Always. Akmed is always busted in."

"Busted out," Ptolemy says automatically. "Do you think he might turn if the price is right?"

"How much is right?"

"I would have to meet him, size him up, see how much it would take to buy him."

"No, that is not possible. To him, you are the enemy. The Great Satan. If I bring you to him, he might kill me and torture my grandmother. No, if it is to be done, you must let me handle it."

The agent stares at him. "I don't have much choice, do I?"

"You must trust me, effendi. I will try to turn Akmed."

"Just keep the baksheesh reasonable. We have deep pockets, but don't get the idea we're Yankee Doodle assholes."

"I will do my best," Youssef says sincerely. "Allah be my judge."

"Uh-huh," Ptolemy says. He rises, pays for Joe's lunch, and leaves the Coney Island Café.

Outside, the afternoon sun strikes like a flamethrower. The agent dodges traffic to cross the street, and ducks into a parked Datsun. He slumps down behind the wheel, panama pulled low, and watches the door of the café. He smokes two English Ovals before Khalidi finally comes out.

Ptolemy is surprised at what happens next. Joe raises his arm, snaps his fingers, and a chauffeured black BMW pulls up. He gathers the skirt of his burnoose and climbs into the back seat. The BMW takes off.

The agent starts the Datsun, makes a wild U-turn that almost causes a riot, with everyone screaming Arabic curses at him ("Your sister fucks camels!"), and takes off after the BMW. He expects to follow Youssef into the Casbah but instead, after a half hour's drive, finds himself in a pleasant suburb of whitewashed villas behind high walls covered with bougainvillea.

The BMW pauses at a handsome wrought-iron gate set in an ornamental fence surrounding at least an acre of manicured lawn. And in the center, a low, rambling house of white stucco with narrow windows and a red tile roof. Khalidi alights, speaks to the chauffeur a moment, then waves the car away.

He unlocks the gate, enters, carefully relocks the gate behind him. Ptolemy, parked on the verge of the paved road fifty yards away, sees his quarry approach a woman seated in a thronelike lawn chair near the front door of the house.

The woman, wearing a black chador, rises with difficulty and stands shakily with the aid of a cane. Ptolemy can see that she is old, old, old. The grandmother, he guesses. She and Youssef talk a few moments, both of them gesturing wildly. Suddenly the gammer begins whacking Joe with her cane, aiming at his legs and buttocks. He cowers away from her and then, as the frantic blows continue to fall, turns and flees into the house. The old woman hobbles after him, brandishing her cane.

Ptolemy waits patiently, finishing his packet of English Ovals. He never takes his eyes from Khalidi's home, but by nightfall there have been no arrivals and no departures. It is obvious that Joe will not be meeting with Akmed that afternoon. Sighing, the agent heads back to Cairo.

There, in the lighted court behind the hotel, he finds Control and Tut, both wearing white flannels, engaged in a lethargic tennis match. When their game is finished, they join Ptolemy at an umbrella table, and all three order Singapore Slings, which seem fitting.

Ptolemy relates the events of his day, including Khalidi's promise to attempt to turn Akmed. Control listens closely, then signals the waiter for another round of drinks.

"Langley has the hots for Operation Soufflé," he says, "but let's move cautiously on this Akmed character until we can establish his *bona fides.*

Let's tell Khalidi that we'll need some verifiable tidbits from Akmed before he can shake the money tree."

"How about this," Tut suggests. "Akmed has to come up with the exact location of Marilyn's eggs. I'll check it with my contact at Shin Bet, and if it proves out, we put Akmed on the payroll."

"Yeah," Control says, "I think that'll fly. Ptolemy, you get the word to Joe as soon as possible. We don't want to drag our feet on this one."

Ptolemy says, "He's going to ask how much we'll pay."

"Five thousand American," Control says promptly. "Tops. And for that we want Akmed, body and soul."

"I'm not sure Akmed will go for it."

"Sure he will," Control says cheerfully. "Five grand will buy a *herd* of clean fat boys."

Manhattan, NY

McBryde's men all agree that sending Sergeant Rumfry to the Staten Island ferry terminal to intercept the white Jaguar was a cute idea; it just didn't work, that's all. Which meant the Jag with the two phony gas inspectors was still on the Island or had returned to Brooklyn or Manhattan via the Verrazano Bridge.

"Or went to Jersey by the Goethals Bridge," Rumfry suggests.

But the lieutenant doesn't want to think about that. He's convinced the theft of Marilyn's eggs was a Big City crime; that's where they were stolen, and that's where they'll be recovered. So he requests help from the New York State Department of Motor Vehicles. When he receives the computer printout showing all the two-door Jaguars registered in the New York City area, his crew groans at the enormity of the task awaiting them.

But when they pull the records of Jaguars registered in Manhattan, and pluck out those with license numbers including the digits 8, 6, and 1, the job seems doable. Rumfry and two officers start pounding the pavement. Two other uniforms begin running the names and addresses of Jag owners through the NYPD Records computer to see if any of them have sheets.

Meanwhile, McBryde has another go-around with Deputy Inspector Gripsholm. The lieutenant confesses he came close with the Yum-Yum decal, but no cigar. Gripsholm isn't happy about the failure and spends twenty minutes spelling out, for the detective's benefit, all the pressure he's under. If McBryde can't show some solid results, and fast, the Deputy may have to take the lieutenant off the case and bring in fresh blood.

"It's your decision," McBryde says stonily. "Sir," he adds. Then: "I think we're close to breaking this, but it's going to take time. If you think someone can move faster, then replace me. I'm not going to pout and stamp my foot."

Gripsholm stares at him morosely. "I'd have jerked you a week ago," he says, "but that Marilyn Taylor got to the Mayor, and through him to the Commissioner. Her majesty wants you to keep handling it, and if you're reassigned, she threatens to raise holy hell with the reporters. You haven't been playing kneesy with that sweet lady, have you?"

"Me?" the detective says. "Fat chance. What would a rich, famous movie star want with a guy on my salary?"

"Beats the hell out of me, unless she's a cop groupie. Stranger things have happened. Now get out of here and go find that Jaguar. This time try to get there before someone else swipes the eggs."

McBryde goes back to his office and starts trying to bring his reports up-to-date. It's not something that has to be done or something he wants to do, but he hopes it will keep him from thinking about Marilyn Taylor and questioning why she saved his ass. Finally he can stand it no longer, pushes all the bumf aside, and calls her town house.

He gets Harriet Boltz, the snotty secretary, who starts giving him a hard time. But then Marilyn breaks in, apparently on an extension.

"Get off the phone, Harry," she orders, "and let me handle this pas-kudnyak. Listen, McBryde, it's really thoughtful of you to call so often and keep me informed on what you're doing to get my eggs back."

"There was no point in calling," he says stiffly. "I have nothing to report."

"Bull*shit!*" she says angrily. "You're doing *something,* aren't you? Well, I want to know what it is. Would you like to end up walking a beat in Bed-Sty? If not, you better get your tuchis over here pronto. I've had a lousy day so far, and I've had to lower the boom on a lot of idiots, so I'm in the mood to set you straight, too. How soon can you get here?"

"Maybe an hour," he says, figuring he owes her.

"That'll do," she says crisply. "On your way over, pick me up a pint of Häagen-Dazs chocolate chocolate chip. I need a fix."

He hurries, too hopeful to wonder what the hell he's doing, and it's not much more than an hour before they're in her frothy bed, naked as needles. He watches her wolf down the ice cream like there's no tomorrow.

"Listen," she says between gulps, "that crap I gave you on the phone—forget it. Harriet was probably listening in, so I had to come on strong."

"That's okay."

"But most of it was true. I've had a miserable day. On the phone for hours. Canned a dozen stupes. My favorite indoor sport. And also, I really do want to know what you've been up to."

"It's a long story."

"I've got all the time in the world."

"All right then, I'll tell you. Just don't interrupt."

"Yes, boss," she says.

So he starts relating the saga of Nicholas Kazanian and the plot hatched at Turk's Bar in Brooklyn. Then the search for the Yum-Yum Burger Shoppe decal and the discovery of Ronald Yates and his Staten Island shrine to Marilyn. And then the bogus gas inspectors in the two-door Jag who grabbed the eggs just minutes before McBryde arrived.

"Whee!" Marilyn says when he finishes. "It sounds like a combination of *The Maltese Falcon* and *Bugs Bunny at the Circus.* Where do you go from here?"

"Try to trace the car and the weirdies who copped your eggs. But I think you'll be hearing from them soon anyway. They sound like a couple of sharp operators out to make a fast buck."

She is silent a moment, pondering. Then: "Tell me something, McBryde: How did those two crazies get to that kid on Staten Island before you did?"

He sighs. "I was afraid you'd ask that. Because I blew it. The way I figure, they were smart enough to realize the original crooks would have to buy extra liquid nitrogen to keep the eggs fresh. So they hit all the places in the New York area that sell the liquefied gas. I should have thought of that in the first place, but I didn't. I'm sorry."

"So you're not perfect after all."

"I never claimed to be."

"Sometimes you act like you think you are. But if you've got luck, you don't have to be perfect; I learned that a long time ago. Listen, you think my eggs are still good?"

"As far as I know. The clowns who have them swiped Yates's extra liquid nitrogen too, and they'll know enough to keep the eggs frozen. It's been stressed in every newspaper story and television report. They'll want to have something to sell back to you."

She puts the empty ice cream carton and spoon on the floor, then turns onto her side to face him. "How come you've never married?" she asks abruptly.

"I've been too busy. How come you've never married?"

"I've been too busy," she says, then sings, "Two busy people by dawn's early light, and too much in love to say good-night. But you want to get married, don't you?"

"Of course. Someday."

"Children, too, I suppose."

"Naturally."

"Naturally," she repeats. "The male ego. You want a son to carry on the McBryde name. Your bid for immortality."

"That's got nothing to do with it. I just happen to like kids. Don't you?"

"No. Smelly monsters."

"The female ego. You're afraid children will interfere with your career. You can't endure the thought of giving up even a little of your independence."

"You couldn't be more wrong."

"I think the correct grammatical form is 'wronger.' "

"I know all about grammar," she says, reaching for him.
They move together, hands busy.
"You have beautiful dangling participles," she murmurs.
"Thank you," he says, "and I love to split your infinitive."

Queens, NY

Rocco Castellano and Vito Zivic sit stolidly in the back room of the steakhouse listening to Morry tell his story.

"So I hit this crazy place on Canal Street that sells all kinds of medical shit. You wouldn't *believe!* The owner, a real putz, wanted a C-note to talk. I coulda busted him up, but I figured live and let live—right? So I leaned on him just a little, and we settle for fifty. He tells me he's had a *parade* asking about liquid nitrogen. The last guys were in yesterday, and he told me the same story he told them: A blond kid wearing a black leather jacket bought a jug of the stuff a coupla days after Marilyn's eggs were snatched. He thinks he was from Staten Island. That any help?"

Rocco stirs restlessly. "Did the putz tell you what the guys who came in yesterday looked like?"

"Yeah, I ast him. Two heavies, and one had a beak like Durante's."

"Thanks, Morry, you done good. Now go out to the bar and get a jolt for yourself."

Castellano waits until the soldier is out of the room, then turns to Vito. "The guy with the bugle—that would be Mario Zucchi. He's ahead of us, so he's either got the eggs now or knows where they are."

"So what do we do, Rocco?"

"First of all, call off the search. Pay everyone and give them chits for a free meal. Then we gotta find out what Mario's up to."

"How can we do that—put the blocks to him?"

"Nah," Rocco Castellano says, grinning, "I think this is a job for Fat Wanda. Give her a call and get her over here."

"Is she out? The last I heard she drew thirty."

"I got it knocked down," Rocco says, "so she owes me. Also, tell her there's a job that'll pay her a bill a day plus expenses; she'll come running."

"Fat Wanda can't run," Zivic says, "but I'll call."

She shows up at the steakhouse at four o'clock that afternoon dressed completely in fire-engine red. Rope a gondola to her ankles and she could qualify in a hot air balloon race. Rocco gets three bottles of beer at the bar and takes her into the back room.

"Where you been keeping yourself, sweetie?" she says. "The girls been asking for you."

"Here and there," Castellano says vaguely. "Jesus, Wanda, you been putting on more weight?"

"Maybe a few pounds. You know what they say: the bigger the cushion, the better the pushin'. Listen, sweetie, thanks for sending the mouthpiece around. He done me real good."

"I hope you paid him."

"Oh, sure," she says demurely, "he got his." She drinks directly from the bottle, wipes her mouth on her sleeve. "Vito says you got a job for me. I could use the kale. Business ain't been so good lately. Too much amateur competition."

"I know what you mean. Look, Wanda, one of the reasons I picked you was because I know you can keep your mouth shut."

"I don't blab," she says, starting on her second bottle of beer.

Rocco tells her all about the theft of Marilyn's eggs, and Mario Zucchi's presence in town.

Fat Wanda is a quick study and doesn't ask any unnecessary questions. "You wanna know if this Zucchi has the eggs awreddy, and if he don't, does he know where they are. Right?"

"You got it," Castellano says approvingly. "Look, the guy's got no legal right to be doing what he's doing. He's out of his territory and shouldn't be operating in New York. I mean it's just not right and proper. If anyone makes a big score from the eggs, it should be the locals. Am I correct?"

"A hunnert percent, sweetie. Where does this guy hang?"

"The Hotel Bedlington in Manhattan. The joint has got a cocktail bar, and Mario likes the sauce, so I figured you could probably pick him up there."

"How will I know him?"

"He's got a nose like a knuckle; you can't miss him. Also, he drinks Chivas and soda."

"Married?"

"Yeah, wife and two kids. But they're on the left coast."

"I get the picture. When do you want me to start?"

"The sooner the better."

"Then I'll get over there tonight. A little token of your esteem?"

"Three bills to get you started. All right?"

"You're a sweetie, sweetie."

"If you have to take a room at the Bedlington, that's okay, too. Just get the guy halfway tanked and he'll sing like a birdie. And listen, Wanda, maybe you better not wear bright red; it might scare him off. Black would be better."

"Don't worry," Fat Wanda says. "I can do class."

Manhattan, NY

Gary Flomm comes into the office where Harriet Boltz is working on the journal she keeps of Marilyn's personal expenses.

"I've got Sam Davidson on the phone," Flomm starts, "and he—"

"Tell him to get lost," Boltz interrupts sharply. "She's not going to read his script or do his film. And that's that."

"Harry, it's not about his script. He claims he's got a lead on the guys who swiped the eggs. And he described the refrigerator flask exactly."

Harriet looks up. "You sure?"

"Absolutely. I think you better talk to him."

"All right, put him on this phone."

Flomm leaves the office, and a moment later Harriet's phone buzzes. She picks up.

"Davidson?"

"Yep."

"Harriet Boltz here. What's this bullshit?"

"It's not bullshit," Sam says. "I know who's got the eggs."

"Who?"

"I want to talk to Marilyn personally."

"No way. You tell me, and I'll tell her."

"Look, I either talk to Marilyn or you can forget I called. Then it's on your head."

Harriet bites her thumbnail. "Give me your number, and I'll check with her and call you back."

"I'm in a pay phone and can't tie it up. I'll call you again in fifteen minutes."

He disconnects, and Boltz goes up to the gym where Marilyn, clad in a fuchsia leotard, is doing aerobics to a tape of the Grateful Dead. Harriet marches over to the player and turns it off.

"What the hell," Marilyn says indignantly.

"Listen to this," her secretary says, and tells her about Sam Davidson's call. "Gary says he described the container exactly. Marilyn, you don't suppose Sam snaffled the eggs himself, do you?"

"Nah. He's a sleazeball, but he hasn't got the moxie for a caper like that."

"So what do you want to do?" Boltz asks. "Talk to him?"

"I guess I better," Marilyn says, sighing. "Get him over here; I'm not going to meet that crumb in a dark alley."

"Maybe you should call McBryde. He might want to listen in on your talk with Davidson, or maybe follow Sam when he leaves."

"No, I'll handle this myself," Marilyn says decisively. "McBryde's on a wild goose chase, trying to track down a Jaguar. If I can get the eggs back myself, maybe it'll teach him a little humility."

"Why would you want to do that?" Harriet asks curiously.

"Oh, I don't know. Sometimes he acts so fucking superior I can't stand it. I'd like to teach him a lesson."

"Uh-huh. You know what I think? I think you're gone on the guy."

"Oh, shut up and tell Davidson I'll deal."

Sam shows up about an hour later, carrying the script of *Private Parts, II* in a brown paper bag and trying desperately to remember the details of the scenario Champ DuBois has created. He is ushered into an office where Marilyn sits in a high-backed swivel chair, big as a throne, and glares at him.

"All right, schmucko," she says, "what's all this about my eggs?"

"Look, doll," he says earnestly, "you know that in our business sometimes you've got to be nice to people who ain't so nice."

"Cruds, you mean."

"Well, yeah, but *rich* cruds. Marilyn, I got to wheel and deal with these guys. So last night I'm having drinks with this moneybags in his apartment, which is just a little smaller than Grand Central Station, and he inhales more thirty-year-old scotch than is good for him and starts babbling about all the big scores he's made. That's when I realize this nogoodnik is an out-and-out thief. I mean he doesn't pull the jobs himself, but he lines them up, hires other thugs to do the dirty work, and takes most of the profits."

"What's his name?"

"I can't tell you that."

"Where's his apartment?"

"I can't tell you that either. Give me a break; I'm trying to save my ass. If he knew I was talking to you, he'd ship me back to the Coast in a gunnysack. What I'm trying to say is that this guy is a heavy."

"So what were you doing with him?"

"Trying to get financing for my film—what else? He's always looking for legit ways to invest his loot. So after he tells me about all the big jobs he's engineered, he starts bragging about the biggest—which is stealing your eggs from the guys who stole them in the first place. He robbed the robbers."

Marilyn begins to think Davidson might be telling the truth. Not *all* the truth—he's incapable of that—but some of it. What he just said ties in with what McBryde told her.

"Did you see my eggs?" she demands.

"Sure, I saw them. They're in the white flask I described to Gary Flomm. And this guy's got a jug of extra liquid nitrogen to keep them frozen."

"And now he wants to collect the hundred thousand dollars I offered for their return—right?"

"Not right," Sam says, trying his best to do sincere. "He's not interested in a hundred grand. He figures he can get a cool million on the black market."

"What!" Marilyn cries. "A million? From whom? What black market?"

"He looked into the whole thing, and he says there are a lot of wealthy infertile women in this country who are looking for eggs. Then they'll have them fertilized with their husband's sperm, and the embryo will be plugged into the woman, and they'll have the kid they always wanted. Made with the famous Marilyn Taylor's genes. They'll pay top bucks for that."

"Godammit!" she yells. "Those eggs are *mine*, and I want them."

"That's what I came to tell you," Davidson says patiently. "You're not going to get them for a hundred grand. Not when he can get so much more peddling them to other people."

"There are only nine eggs," Marilyn says hotly. "That was in all the papers. This jerko thinks he can get more than a hundred thousand an egg?"

Sam shrugs. "That's what he figures. And maybe he's right. Every rich, childless couple will think that with your egg they'll get a kid as beautiful and talented as you."

She rises abruptly, stalks fretfully about the office, arms crossed, hugging her elbows. "I can't believe this. Suddenly I'm a filly waiting for nine studs."

"Look, they don't call you The Most Beautiful Woman in the World for nothing. Your eggs are the best, strictly world-class. You gotta know that."

Still she strides, conscious of the blatant flattery but unable to resist it. "A million," she repeats, thinking that if she hadn't had tubal ligation she could be popping an egg a month. She estimates annual income. Not bad. And without all the hassle of running a financial empire.

"I just wanted to tell you all this," Davidson goes on, "so you know where you stand. You'll never get them back for a hundred thousand."

She stops suddenly, turns to look at him. "Half?" she says hopefully. "Will the shtarker return them for half a million?"

Sam frowns. "I doubt it. If you want me to, I'll try. You want me to try?"

"Yes," Marilyn Taylor says determinedly. "Try."

"Okay," he says, rising. "I'll give it my best shot. You know how I feel about you. Like you're my own daughter."

"God forbid!" she says. Then, when he starts out the door, she calls after him: "Hey! You forgot your package."

"Oh, that," he says lightly. "It's the script of *Private Parts, Two.* Maybe you'll get a chance to look at it while I'm going to bat for you."

She stares at him a moment. "Oh-ho," she says, "now I get it. You're using the eggs as blackmail to get me to do your lousy film."

"Not blackmail," he protests. "It's just you scratch my back and I'll scratch yours."

"I wouldn't scratch your back with rubber gloves," she says bitterly.

Manhattan, NY

All the wiseguys in Chicago know the man called Shakespeare, but few know his real monicker: Loring Minchley Flotsom. He was what critics called a "promising" actor until he discovered the glories of airplane glue. After scrambling Hamlet's soliloquy one night ("bare bodkin" came out as "bod barekin"), his career went rapidly downhill. But he didn't much care, having substituted nose candy for glue.

But the bentnoses found ways to use his thespian talents. He can play a hundred different roles and is a genius with disguises and dialects. Now he's employed as front man in stock swindles, real estate frauds, and occasionally in heavier stuff like extortion, counterfeiting, forgery, and shakedowns of corporate execs who neglect to ask the age of the nymphets helpfully supplied by the mob.

He is a tall, willowy man who favors long hair and Lord Byron shirts. When he shows up at Mario Zucchi's suite at the Hotel Bedlington, he's wearing the poet's shirt under a black silk suit with glass eyes used as buttons. There is also a sprig of edelweiss pinned to his lapel.

Mario offers him a drink, but Shakespeare declines. "Never touch the stuff," he says, pale nose twitching. "Rusts the pipes, y'know."

"Where you staying?" Zucchi says. "Here at the hotel?"

"Oh, dear me, no. This place seems a bit *infra dig,* wouldn't y'say? No, I'm bunking with an old school chum who owns a rather modest town house on Gramercy Park."

"Is he in the game?" The Nose asks anxiously.

"It's a she, old boy, and, no, she is not in the game. But perfectly safe, I do assure you. Spends all her time embroidering portraits of the presidents on footstools. She's already up to Millard Fillmore. A sweet but rather dotty lady. Magnificent embonpoint."

"Yeah?" Zucchi says. "What's that?"

"Tits. Listen, old boy, The Man filled me in on this little project of yours. I'll need a car and a driver."

"You got 'em. Rent the kind of car you want, and for a driver I'll give you Dino, one of my boys. He's got a lot of muscle, including between his ears, but he's a good kid and can take orders."

"Excellent. I intend to reconnoiter the apartment house where Marilyn's eggs are being held and then determine my *modus operandi.*"

"You do that," Mario says, "and also figure out how you want to work it."

Shakespeare looks at him. "Yes," he says, and departs.

This is in the late afternoon, and when Shakespeare doesn't return or call in, Zucchi reckons he's gone to Gramercy Park for dinner with his dotty lady. So he cabs down to Little Italy and has a great steak pizzaiola at a joint on Mott Street. The house wine, probably made in the basement, is sharp enough to clean an engine block.

By the time Mario returns uptown, he's feeling no pain and stops in the hotel's cocktail lounge for a nightcap or two. The place is practically empty: just a young couple with their heads together in a dim corner and a lady wearing black seated at the bar. She's a large one, and Zucchi wonders how she was able to hoist her bulk onto a bar stool.

The Nose puts his foot on the polished brass rail and orders a Chivas, seltzer on the side. It goes down so smoothly that he orders a second, then says to the bartender in a lordly manner, "And ask the lady if she will allow me to buy her a drink."

She turns to look at him. "Thank you, kind sir," she says, "but only if you let me get the next round."

"Why not?" he says, and takes the stool next to her. He watches the bartender pour their drinks. "Hey, you're drinking Chivas, too. You've got good taste."

"I like to go first class," she says.

He nods approvingly. "There's no other way. Life is short—right?"

She lifts her glass in a toast. "Short and merry," she says.

"I'll drink to that," Mario says, and does.

Five minutes later they're telling each other the stories of their lives, somewhat embellished.

"I'm in import-export," he says. "What do you do?"

"I'm a physical therapist," she says.

"No kidding? You mean like massage?"

"When it's called for. Also exercise, heat, and other forms of stimulation, depending on the needs of the individual requiring treatment. For instance, I'd guess you are a man under a lot of stress, a lot of pressure."

He looks at her with amazement. "You got me dead to rights."

She reaches up to feel the muscle between his neck and shoulder. "Tense trapezius," she says, "definitely tense. You're all knotted up."

"Yeah," he says, "I am. Hey, my name is Mario. What's yours?"

"Wanda."

"You live in New York, Wanda?"

"No, I'm from Scranton. I just came up for a few days to do a little shopping."

"Where you staying?"

"Right here in the hotel."

"Uh-huh," he says. "Me, too. Let's have another round. And this is all on me."

"Whatever you say, Mario."

They sit at the bar for another two hours. She matches him drink for drink, but it seems to have no effect on her, while he is conscious of getting plotched. When they rise to leave, he staggers a bit and she puts a warm hand on his arm to steady him.

"It's the stress I'm under," he tells her. "Pressure. I'm tense. All knotted up."

"Poor baby," she says. "You need shiatsu."

"Yeah? What's that?"

"I'll show you," she says. "What's your room number?"

He's got a bottle in his suite and continues drinking while she gets him undressed and starts working on him with her strong fingers.

"Oh, boy," he murmurs. "Oh, boy."

"So tell me," she says, refilling his glass, "why all the stress? Why is your gluteus maximus so hard?"

He begins mumbling, and she leans closer to listen. She continues working on him, keeping his glass filled, until he passes out. Then she undresses and gets into bed next to him.

During the night he stirs and jabs her awake with a sharp elbow.

"Was it as good for you as it was for me?" he asks muzzily.

"Better," she assures him.

Manhattan, NY

The search for the white two-door Jaguar is donkeywork, going so slowly that Lieutenant McBryde is able to persuade Gripsholm to assign him more men.

"It's the only lead we've got," he argues, "and it needs manpower if we're ever going to break it. You're still getting pushed, aren't you?"

"Don't ask," the Deputy Inspector says sadly. "The funny thing is that suddenly The Goddess of the Silver Screen isn't making waves. All the flak is coming from political assholes who want to be on TV when the eggs are recovered. All right, I'll give you two more uniforms. If this keeps up, we'll have a permanent Egg Squad. I don't even want to think about how much money the Department has spent on this mishegas."

"Maybe Marilyn will make a contribution if we get her eggs back."

"Oh, yeah," Gripsholm says. "When bears stop shitting in the woods."

They finally winnow the computer printout down to nine questionable Jaguar owners in Manhattan. Four of the nine have police records, but it's all minor stuff—like screaming obscenities at a traffic cop who wrote out a ticket and then said, "Have a nice day."

McBryde works as hard as his crew: ringing doorbells, invading apartments and town houses, tracing owners to offices and weekend homes in the country. After days of this, they are left with three possibles.

But Oliver Hibbard turns out to be a tax attorney working in the offices of an investment banker on Wall Street. He's sixty-four, and as Sergeant Rumfry says, his age and waistband match. It's hard to believe an old roly-poly like that would take a jaunt to Staten Island to glom Marilyn's eggs.

And Reggie Schlemmer is a fashion photographer who, under questioning, seems freaky enough to have pulled the caper. But investigation proves that on the day Ronald Yates was robbed of his treasure, the photographer was shooting brassieres in Madagascar.

Lieutenant Jeffrey McBryde, beginning to wonder if he's chasing butterflies, decides to track down the third subject himself. The guy lives in an apartment house on Park Avenue.

The name on his vehicle registration is Moses Leroy Washington.

Queens, NY

Fat Wanda has her feet parked up on Castellano's desk in the back room of the steakhouse. There's an empty bottle of suds in front of her, and she's working on a second.

"You gotta know Mario was swacked," she tells Rocco and Vito Zivic. "I mean blotto. So he wasn't making a helluva lot of sense. But he kept mumbling about this million-dollar deal he was working on."

"Did he mention the eggs?" Rocco wants to know.

"Never said word one about them. Just that he was going to make this big score."

"Did he say when?" Zivic asks.

"I got the feeling it's going to be in the next few days, a week at the most. Sorry I couldn't get more but like I say, the guy was stewed to the gills. Oh, yeah, one other thing: A couple times he mentioned Shakespeare. 'Me and Shakespeare' and 'Shakespeare is working for me now.' Does that mean anything to you?"

Rocco looks at Vito. "Yeah," he says, "it means something. Shakespeare is a slick con man working out of Chicago. They call him that because he used to be an actor, but now he's a dusthead. If he's in town, it means The Man sent him to help Zucchi take the eggs."

"Well," Wanda says, finishing her beer, "I did the best I could. You want me off the job?"

"No," Castellano says, "you stay on. Keep cozying up to Mario and see if you can find out when the action is going down."

"Whatever you say, Rocco. I got me a room at the Bedlington so I won't have to travel back and forth."

Castellano ponders a moment. "Tell you what," he says finally, "keep an eye out for Shakespeare. He's a tall, skinny guy with long hair and he never wears a necktie. Maybe you'll spot him with Mario or hanging around the hotel. If you make him, give me or Vito a call right away, and we'll send Morry over to tail him. This Shakespeare is a real cute operator, and I'm betting he's running the show, not Zucchi."

"Okay, sweetie," she says, rising. "I'll get back to Manhattan. Mario wants me to have dinner with him tonight."

"That's nice," Rocco says, grinning. "Now you got a good job and all you can eat."

"I know what you mean," Fat Wanda says.

Manhattan, NY

"I'll need a big car," Shakespeare says to Dino. "Massive but not ostentatious."

So they rent a silver Cadillac Brougham and drive over to a theatrical costumer on Tenth Avenue. The goon stays behind the wheel of the double-parked car while the actor climbs worn wooden steps to an enormous third-floor loft. The place is jammed with racks and bins of costumes, wigs, masks, and beards.

"May I help you?" asks Dr. Frankenstein's monster.

Shakespeare glances around. The other clerks are Napoleon, a dwarfish pirate, and a skinny black woman wearing a Richard Nixon mask.

"Something for a masquerade party," Shakespeare says. "Unusual y'know."

"We got it," the monster says. "How about Roger Rabbit? Mickey Mouse? Woody Woodpecker?"

"Oh, dear me, no. A little more dignified than that."

"I can give you a great Abraham Lincoln with beard, stovepipe hat, and stick-on mole."

"Sorry, won't do. Perhaps something religious."

"How about Jesus with a big balsa cross?"

" 'Fraid not."

"We gotta sensational Pope. We gotta dynamite Gandhi. We gotta socko John the Baptist. It looks like you got no head, but you carry this fake head around on a silver tray."

"Fascinatin' but a bit awkward, y'know. Perhaps I should be a Catholic priest. Black dickey, starched white collar—that sort of thing."

"We can provide," the monster says, "but it's got no pizzazz. Listen, how would you like to be a Hasidic Jew? We've got your long black coat, your wide-brimmed fur hat, your sausage curls that hang down. Best of all, you don't gotta stick the curls on with gum or tape; they're attached to the hat."

"Excellent!" Shakespeare cries. "May I try it on?"

"Of course. And with it we supply your heavy horn-rimmed specs with plain glass."

"Better and better."

A half hour later, having inspected himself in a three-way mirror and being delighted with the transformation, Shakespeare pays cash for costume rental and the deposit required.

"I need your name and address," the monster says.

"Mario Zucchi. The Hotel Bedlington on Madison Avenue."

He carries the big packages down to the Cadillac.

"We're in business," he tells Dino.

They return to the hotel. Dino carries the packages up to Zucchi's suite. Shakespeare glances into the cocktail lounge. Mario is seated at the bar with a robust woman. He sees Shakespeare and beckons, but the actor smiles and turns away.

"Who was that?" Fat Wanda asks.

"A guy who works for me," Zucchi says. "But he don't drink."

"What's he," Wanda says, "mentally retarded or something? Hey, I gotta visit the little girls' room. Be right back."

She finds a public phone on the lobby mezzanine. She calls the steakhouse and talks to Vito Zivic.

"Listen," she says, "you better get Morry over here right away. I just spotted Shakespeare."

Boston, MA

The monsignor and the professor are half in the bag and enjoying every minute of it.

"Terry," Farthingale says, "the last time we spoke, I believe I termed the theft of Marilyn's eggs a crime against humanity and suggested that the United Nations might be the proper organization to investigate the offense."

"And then prosecute the perpetrators if and when they are apprehended."

"Exactly. But my feeling now is that the theft of Marilyn's eggs would come under the jurisdiction of the International Court of Justice, which is the judicial arm of the United Nations, only upon petition of members of the General Assembly, the Security Council, or any other international agency authorized to so petition."

"Dear Hiram," the monsignor says benignly, "would you tell me in layman's language—if that is possible—exactly what your comments signify and where your argument is heading."

"It occurred to me," the professor continues, "that a petition to the World Court to adjudicate the theft of Marilyn's eggs would be seriously considered by the Court if it were to be presented by the Vatican."

O'Dell reaches for the cognac decanter, refills his glass and his host's as well. "The Vatican?" he said hoarsely.

"Precisely. Because the theft is, as we agree, an offense against all mankind."

"An intriguing proposal," the monsignor says thoughtfully. "Very intriguing."

"Then you don't reject it out of hand?"

"By no means. I believe there is good reason to hope that the Holy See might conceivably wish to use the theft of Marilyn's eggs in an effort to awaken the conscience of the world. But you must realize, old friend, that the Vatican has, to my knowledge, no capability of investigating a crime of this nature."

"I didn't think they had," Farthingale says.

"Then what agency might conduct an investigation that would convince the Vatican to petition the International Court of Justice?"

The professor stares at him with a secret smile. The monsignor is puzzled a moment, then his broad face relaxes into an admiring grin.

"Oh, Hiram," he says, "what a sly old fox you are! You are proposing that the Vatican, through an emissary, makes a top secret and very subtle appeal to the White House, requesting that our Federal Bureau of Investigation look into the theft of Marilyn's eggs, with the promise that, if the case is solved, it will be brought before the World Court by the Vatican."

"I knew I could count on your discernment. It would earn brownie points for all concerned: the Vatican, White House, FBI, and World Court."

O'Dell nods. "I still have some friends in Rome. Surely it would do no harm to make a few discreet inquiries as to the curia's interest in your proposal."

"No, no," Farthingale protests, holding up a palm. "More of a suggestion than a proposal."

"Whatever you wish to call it," the monsignor says, "it *reeks* of genius!"

"Thank you," the professor says humbly.

Manhattan, NY

Mutha is behind the bar mixing a shaker of Blue Devil cocktails. The Chin twins are seated on the tiled floor of the foyer playing a game of jacks. Champ DuBois is lounging in his favorite chair. Sam Davidson is perched on a bar stool, listening warily to the maniac's lecture.

"Everything in moderation," DuBois proclaims. "I am greedy, you are greedy, the world is greedy. But immoderate greed can only lead to disappointment and, possibly, a kick in the ass. You dig?"

"Oh, yeah," Sam says. "Sure."

"Now we could hold out for a million for Marilyn's eggs. But the lady has bid a half-mil. From what I've read about her, she is a ballsy female who rebels when she feels she's being jerked around. So I suggest you tell her that your principal is a reasonable man, ambitious but not greedy. Tell her you have been able to persuade me to reduce the ransom to eight hundred thousand. If she continues to bleat, you are authorized to come down to seven-fifty, but no lower. Is that perfectly clear?"

Sam nods, wondering how many years in the slam are awarded to involuntary accomplices in criminal activities.

"Now as to method of payment . . . I will accept a teller's check providing Marilyn is willing to wait until the check is cashed before the eggs are returned."

"And who should the check be made out to?"

DuBois displays his incisors. "You, of course."

"Oh, God!" Davidson cries. "That'll put me in deep shit. After the eggs are returned, the buttons will come looking for me."

"Never fear," Champ says. "Marilyn won't agree to the scheme. She's too sharp for that, fearing the check will be cashed but the eggs won't be returned. Then you tell her the only other option is cash. Nothing over a hundred-dollar note. All used bills, and no numbers in sequence."

"It's going to take her awhile to get that kind of loot from a bank."

"So? I'm a patient man. When she informs you that the cash is ready, I will give you instructions as to the time and place of the exchange. Now I suggest you give the lady a call and make an appointment."

Davidson calls, and, after being shunted from Gary Flomm to Harriet Boltz to Marilyn, is told that she will see him between noon and one o'clock. He reports this to DuBois.

"Excellent! I'm sure she's as eager as I to bring this enterprise to a successful and mutually satisfactory conclusion. Mutha, did you catch that language? Wasn't it *noble!*"

"Yeth, mutha," Mutha says.

"So off you go, Sam," Champ says. "Mutha and I are leaving shortly to view a mouth-watering exhibit of precious gems at the Museum of Natural History. Perhaps they're giving out samples."

"Ho-ho, boss, that's rich," Davidson says.

"Return here after your meeting with Marilyn and wait for us. I'm most anxious to learn when the funds will be available."

Sam leaves the Park Avenue apartment and plods over to Marilyn's town house. Reflecting on his mission and its probable outcome, he wonders if a New York judge would accept residence in Hollywood as *prima facie* evidence of insanity.

But his fears of a world-class balls-up are mitigated by Marilyn's manner. She meets him in the living room, and Attila the Huness is all sweetness. She even serves him a diet cola.

"And it's got no caffeine," she tells him.

"Gee, that's keen," he says. "I certainly wouldn't want to stay awake tonight."

He then launches into Champ DuBois's script, and to his surprise Marilyn agrees to everything. She doesn't even try to chisel him down to seven-fifty. She'll pay eight hundred thousand dollars for the return of her eggs, no questions asked, and will let Sam know as soon as the cash is available.

She's so accommodating, in fact, that he begins to get uneasy. "Hey, doll," he says suspiciously, "that's a lot of lettuce. You're treating it like it's bubkes. You must really want those eggs back."

"Oh, Sam," she says lightly, "it's only money. Sure, I want my eggs back, but that's not the only reason I'm willing to pay."

"No? What's the other reason?"

"Don't you know?" she says, staring at him with those big azure eyes that have driven men mad with longing. "It's your script, honey. It's *Private Parts, Two.* Sam, I read it and it's a guaranteed winner. That's why I want to cooperate—to keep you happy so I can do your movie."

"No kidding?" he says. "You really like it?"

"Like it?" she says. "I *love* it! Of course I want a few more scenes, some beefed-up dialogue."

"Naturally," he says happily. "Whatever you ask for, you'll get. Believe me, that script will be just the way you want it before we shoot a single frame."

"Oh, Sam," she says, putting a warm hand over his, "it'll be so great working with you again. But let's get this egg business out of the way first, and then it's full speed ahead."

"Right!" he shouts. "Full speed ahead! I'll keep calling until you tell me the cash is ready. Then you get your eggs back, and we go into production."

"I can hardly wait," she says.

After he leaves, she flops back onto the couch and kicks her heels high in the air in a paroxysm of glee. "Schmuckooo!" she howls. Then she summons Harriet and tells her the good news.

"He went for it," she reports. "The conniving idiot! If he had a brain, he'd be dangerous."

"You're going to pack a suitcase with cut newspaper, of course."

"Don't tell me how to do it," Marilyn says. "I played the same role in *The Guilty Saint*—remember? We'll nab Sam when he shows up with the eggs and find out who's behind him. Now's the time to call McBryde and have him set up the trap. Is that smartass cop going to get a shock when he hears I've solved his case for him."

But when Boltz calls McBryde, she's told the lieutenant is not in his office and it's not known when he'll return.

Manhattan, NY

Early in the afternoon, McBryde pulls up on the east side of Park and eyes the apartment house across the avenue. It's a slab of stainless steel with a canopy of etched glass. But the potted trees on the sidewalk are plastic ginkgoes. McBryde leaves his dusty blue Plymouth double-parked and dodges through traffic to the west side.

The doorman is dressed like a Ruritanian admiral. The detective shows his badge and ID.

"I'm looking for a tenant named Moses Leroy Washington," he says.

The doorman shakes his head. "No one here by that name."

"You sure?"

"Sure, I'm sure. I know everyone in the building."

"Uh-huh," McBryde says. "Any of your tenants drive a white two-door Jaguar?"

The admiral hesitates.

"Make it easy on yourself," the detective says softly. "You don't want to get racked up for obstruction of justice, do you?"

"I don't want to get racked up for *anything.*"

"So?"

"Yeah, we got a tenant drives a white Jag."

"Two-door?"

Nod.

"And what's his name?"

"Champ DuBois."

"Very nice. Is he in right now?"

"No, I seen him drive away a couple hours ago."

"What's he look like?"

"A tall, skinny black. Dresses with a lot of flash."

"Sure he does," McBryde says genially. "Does he live alone?"

"He's got like a butler who lives in."

"A butler?"

"Sort of."

"He wouldn't be an Oriental who wears black silk pajamas, would he?"

"Sometimes," the doorman says cautiously. "The two of them dress crazy."

"Anyone else live in the apartment?"

Again the doorman hesitates.

"Come on," the detective says. "I don't want to pull you in and crush your kidneys with a rubber hose just to get a few answers."

"You kidding?" the doorman says, aghast.

"Yeah, I'm kidding," McBryde says. "Now who else lives in this apartment with Champ DuBois?"

"I think he's got these two young chicks up there."

"He does, huh? Black? White? Hispanic?"

"Chinese."

"That's a regular United Nations he's got there, isn't it?" the lieutenant says pleasantly. "You have a phone I can use?"

"Yeah, but there won't be any trouble, will there?"

"Why should there be any trouble?" McBryde says. "This is just a social visit. Now where's that phone?"

He calls Sergeant Rumfry, gives him the address, and tells him to get uptown as soon as possible.

"Use your wailer if you have to," he says, "but I want you here fast. And bring a couple of uniforms. This may be a mob scene."

"On my way," Rumfry says.

McBryde goes out onto the sidewalk again. "If DuBois shows up," he tells the doorman, "don't bother telling him that a cop's been asking questions."

He returns to the Plymouth and sits behind the wheel, never taking his eyes from the entrance to the apartment house across Park.

Manhattan, NY

Dino carries the packages down from Mario Zucchi's suite at the Hotel Bedlington. Shakespeare is already in the back seat of the Cadillac Brougham, and as they head for the Park Avenue apartment house, the actor begins putting on his costume.

"Just one more run-through, old boy," he says to Dino. "There is a doorman and elevator operator. Then, up in the apartment, we have Champ DuBois and his houseman. Plus two young tarts. The goodies are white plastic jugs with handles, one small, one large. Correct?"

"You got it," his driver says. "Also, that guy I been tailing, that Sam Davidson, might be up in the apartment, too. He spends a lot of time there."

"Dear me," Shakespeare says. "Quite an audience."

"Listen," Dino says anxiously, "you carrying a piece?"

"Oh, I have a dinky .22," the actor says negligently. "A nickel-plated starter's pistol. Unloaded, of course. I loathe violence."

"You never know," Dino says darkly.

When they arrive, Shakespeare orders the Cadillac double-parked around the corner, between Park and Madison. He steps from the car and stands at the driver's open window.

"How do I look?" he asks.

Dino stares with amazement at the wide-brimmed fur hat, long black coat, horn-rimmed glasses, sausage curls hanging down the actor's cheeks. "You could fool me," he marvels.

"I would hope so," Shakespeare says. "Now be a good lad and keep the motor running. When I reappear, we'll want to leave these environs as quickly as possible—within the limits of the law, of course. Turn north on Madison or go over to Fifth Avenue and turn south, depending on the traffic lights. As I told you, our eventual destination is Gramercy Park."

"What if I get rousted by the cops while I'm double-parked?"

"Tell them you are waiting to drive a *very* pregnant lady to the hospital. If that doesn't work, simply drive around the block and double-park here again. You understand your cues?"

"Oh, sure. I'll be here."

"Splendid. Now tell me to 'break a leg.' "

"Why would you want to break a leg?"

Shakespeare sighs. "See you shortly," he says.

He stalks around the corner to Park Avenue with a deliberate, almost magisterial stride. His hands are clasped behind his back, and his head is bowed, apparently in religious meditation. Actually, he is dreaming that *The New York Times*'s drama critic is present to catch this performance.

He approaches the doorman, a stubby man as outrageously caparisoned as he.

"I beg your pardon, my dear sir," Shakespeare says in an accent that's a horrible amalgam of Jackie Mason, Menashe Skulnick, and Mickey Katz. "May I please to have a word with you?"

The Ruritanian admiral stares at him. "Sure, father," he says. "What's on your mind."

"You have in this fine building perhaps a tenant, Mr. Champ DuBois?"

The doorman is startled. "Why, yeah, padre," he says slowly, "we got a tenant by that name. But he's out right now."

"So?" the actor says. "He told me he might be a little late but I should go up to his apartment and wait for him there. He has left word with his sisters to let me in."

"His *sisters?* Well, yeah, I guess that would be okay. If you can't trust a deacon, who can you trust—am I right? The elevator operator will show you where it is."

"Thank you, my dear sir. May the blessings of a beneficent providence be granted to you and your loved ones."

"Thanks, reverend."

Lieutenant McBryde has watched this exchange from across Park Avenue and idly wonders what reason a member of the Hasidim might have to enter that glittery building.

The door to DuBois's apartment is opened by Sam Davidson, who blinks at the visitor with some surprise.

"Please, my dear sir," Shakespeare says, "I have an appointment with Mr. Champ DuBois, and I have been told to wait here for his return."

"He didn't say anything about it," Sam says, "but I guess it's okay. Come on in. Can I take your coat and hat?"

"No, no," the actor says hastily, "it is against my religion."

He follows Sam into the living room where Louella and Loretta Chin are arm wrestling at the bar.

"Good afternoon, young ladies," Shakespeare says somberly, then leans close to Davidson and whispers: "Please, dear sir, may I use your sanitary facilities?"

"What? Oh, you mean the john. Sure, right down the hall there and to your right."

The actor bangs the door of the bathroom behind him, waits a moment, then reopens it softly. He listens and hears the man talking to the two bimbos in the living room. He moves through the rear of the apartment swiftly and quietly. He finds the flasks almost immediately, on a bearskin rug in a small bedroom garishly decorated with crimson silk and a painting of a snarling tiger on black velvet.

He leaves the jugs there and continues his exploration. He finds what he's seeking: a walk-in closet in what is apparently the master bedroom. At least there's an oil painting of a nude Hitler over the bed, one hand hiding his privates, the other raised in the Nazi salute.

"Depraved," Shakespeare murmurs.

The closet door has no lock, but there is a heavy oaken chair nearby that can easily be tilted and jammed under the knob. It will suffice for the time required. The actor unbuttons his heavy overcoat, takes the shiny pistol from the side pocket of his sports jacket: a horrendous plaid tweed that looks as if it needs a shave.

Holding the pistol casually, muzzle pointing downward, he goes back into the living room. Davidson and the Chin twins look up as he enters. Sam is the first to notice the gun.

"Hey," he says, more curious than frightened, "what is that thing?"

"A deadly weapon," Shakespeare says, dropping the Yiddish accent. "Loaded with armor-piercing bullets that can cause grievous harm to human tissue."

"What *is* this?" Davidson demands.

"Haven't time to explain, old boy," the actor says. "The three of you precede me into the back bedroom. And please, no screams, shouts, or weeping. Civility must be maintained."

He points his handgun and, as they look nervously over their shoulders, herds them into the master bedroom. There he directs them into the closet. He closes the door and jams the chair under the knob.

"There is a wide opening at the bottom," he calls to them. "You will have a plentiful supply of air so that claustrophobic anxieties are not warranted. Ta-ta."

Then he pockets his pistol, buttons his overcoat, picks up the two plastic jugs and leaves the apartment. He rings for the elevator and waits calmly.

While Shakespeare is waiting, Detective Lieutenant McBryde stands alongside his Plymouth talking to Sergeant Rumfry and the two uniformed police officers who have just pulled up in a squad car.

"There are two males, two females," he tells them. "Tall, skinny black; old Asian; two young Chinese girls. We hold them all while we toss the apartment for Marilyn's eggs."

"We got no warrant," Rumfry reminds him.

"Screw the warrant," McBryde says. "We've got all the probable cause in the world. The honcho, the black named Champ DuBois, is out right now. So we wait until he comes back. You all know how to wait, don't you? He's driving a —"

As he briefs them, he's been keeping an eye on the entrance to the apartment house across Park Avenue. Suddenly he breaks off.

"My God," he says excitedly, "there's the two-door Jaguar now. Let's go take them."

The others turn to look. A white Jag has pulled up at the etched glass canopy. Champ DuBois gets out first, followed by Mutha. But before the police can move, a man in the traditional clothes of a Hasidic Jew exits from the building carrying a plastic jug in each hand. He takes one look at the guy getting out of the Jaguar and starts running up Park Avenue.

"What the hell?" McBryde shouts. "Let's go!"

But the traffic is thick and they can't get across. One of the uniforms starts blowing his whistle and holding up his hand, but the maniacal drivers ignore him. Cursing, the cops can only watch the action on the other side.

The Hasid gallops wildly, curls tossing on the breeze, long coat flapping out behind him, the plastic containers banging against his knees. And after a shocked moment, DuBois and Mutha dash after him, Champ screaming, "Stop thief!"

The Hasid disappears around the corner, still running. His pursuers pound after him. And finally the lights change, McBryde and his crew go sprinting across. But all they see are DuBois and his houseman standing dejectedly on the sidewalk, watching a Cadillac Brougham zip westward to Fifth Avenue.

"Collar them," McBryde orders. "Then we'll go up to their apartment and arrest everyone in sight. Oh, God, how am I going to explain this to Gripsholm? He'll have my gizzard."

Cairo, Egypt

The belly dancer shimmying on the dance floor of the Coney Island Café has a naval spacious enough, Ptolemy estimates, to hold two boiled shrimp and a dollop of Crosse & Blackwell cocktail sauce. With an effort he turns back to Youssef Khalidi, who is sucking the meat from a braised oxtail.

"Akmed took the money?" the CIA agent asks in a low voice.

Joe nods, spitting bits of gristle onto the floor.

"So? What do we get for our five grand?"

Khalidi sits back, wipes his mouth on the sleeve of his striped djellaba, takes a swig of arrack, helps himself to one of Ptolemy's English Ovals. "Eight kilometers southeast of Sidon," he says quietly, "is a small mountain. It is called, in English, Camel's Hump. On the south side of this mountain is an ancient cave. There are bones in that cave centuries old. Also empty Coca-Cola cans."

"Yes, yes," the agent says impatiently, "I get the picture. And Marilyn's eggs are being held in the cave?"

Youssef nods again. "Far back in the cave. Guarded."

"How many guards?"

"Ten at least, perhaps more. There are also women and children. Members of the Arm of God travel with their families."

"Women and children? That complicates things. Does everyone live in the cave?"

"No. Tents have been set up nearby. Only the guards are in the cave."

"Armed, I suppose."

"Oh, yes."

"Automatic weapons?"

"Kalashnikovs."

"Oh, boy. What about mortars and grenades?"

"They have those also. And machine guns."

"A lot of muscle there," Ptolemy says, frowning. "Some good men are going to die."

"The young die good," Khalidi says sadly.

"No, no," the agent says. "It's 'The good die young.' "

"You are certain of this?"

"Of course."

"But why should the good die young?"

"I don't know why!" the CIA man says angrily. "That's just the saying: 'The good die young.' "

"But I have known some evil young men who have died. And also some good men who have lived many years."

Ptolemy buries his face in his hands for a moment, then looks up, sighing. "Let's just skip it, Joe," he says. "How long will Marilyn's eggs be in the cave at Camel's Hump?"

Youssef thinks a moment. "A week," he offers. "Perhaps two weeks. No longer. Then they will be moved again."

The agent stands. "Not much time," he says. "I better report immediately."

"Don't forget to pay for my lunch," Khalidi says.

Ptolemy finds Control in the cocktail lounge of his hotel, shaking dice with the barman to see who will pay for the next vodka stinger. The agent motions, and his chief joins him at a secluded corner table.

"About Operation Soufflé . . . ," the agent begins, and then repeats what he has heard from Khalidi.

"So Akmed took the bait," Control says with satisfaction. "I knew he would. But I don't like the setup. Too much firepower."

"A jump team?" Ptolemy suggests. "A high-voltage excursion."

"I don't think so," Control says thoughtfully. "Then the problem is how to get our Rambos out of Lebanon. Too many blackhats in that neck of the woods. No, I think copters are the answer. A night hit. Get in fast, neutralize the baddies, grab the eggs, and take off."

"Copters," Ptolemy repeats. "Yes, that makes sense. But we'll have to liaise with the Israelis on that."

"Not necessarily," Control says. "We have units of the Sixth Fleet with attack choppers. We'll be in and out before Shin Bet knows what's happening. I'll get a rocket off to Langley. If they give it the green, we're on our way. Now let's move back to the bar. This is my lucky day."

Manhattan, NY

Deputy Inspector Gripsholm looks at McBryde for a long moment, then turns to stare out the window. "You know," he says, "the last time I cried was when I saw the bills for my daughter's wedding. But I'm fighting back the tears now."

"You can't feel any worse than I do, sir," the lieutenant says mournfully. "We were *that* close. Another two minutes we'd have had Marilyn's eggs. Now all we've got are the jerkos who swiped them from Staten Island —and what the hell can we charge them with?"

"Did you get a good look at the getaway car?"

"Nope. It was a Cadillac—but that's no help."

"So we're back to square one."

"Not exactly. That Hasidic Jew who ran away with the eggs—I talked to Sol Applebaum, one of my temps, and he says there's *no* way a Hasid would touch a woman's eggs, not even with a twenty-foot pole. Those guys are so strict they don't even want women driving their school buses. Also, the doorman says our Jew talked with a thick Yiddish accent. But Sam Davidson, the man we found in the apartment closet, says the Hasid talked with an accent until he pulled his shooter. Then he talked like a fruity Wasp, according to Davidson."

"So?" Gripsholm says. "What does all that add up to?"

"That guy was a phony, dressed like an orthodox member of the Hasidim to get by the doorman and into DuBois's apartment. No one is going to suspect a religious man would have any criminal intent. And it worked. He waltzed past the doorman and into the apartment. The clever sonofabitch!"

"How did he know the eggs were there?"

"I have no idea. We'll find that out when we find *him.*"

"And how do you figure to do that?"

"Look, the perp was wearing a long black overcoat, a wide-brimmed fur hat, and had fake curls. Where do you get an outfit like that? Probably from a place that rents costumes for stage plays and masquerade parties. So I've got Sergeant Rumfry calling every costumer in the New York area, trying to find out if any of them rented a Hasidic outfit in the last week or so."

"Lots of luck," the Inspector says sourly. "I think you're chasing your tail."

"It's all we've got," McBryde argues. "It's worth a shot."

He goes back to his office and finds four messages from Marilyn Taylor. *"Important." "Urgent." "Crucial." "Top priority."* Sighing, he calls the town house.

"Where the hell have you been?" she yells at him. "You get over here right away!"

"What's it about?"

"It's about getting my eggs back, dummy. If you're not here within the hour, I'm calling the Mayor and dumping on you."

"Oh, golly gee," he whines piteously, "please don't do that."

"Stuff it!" she says sharply. "Just get your ass up here pronto."

She meets him in the living room. She's wearing a luscious lime silk jumpsuit and looks like a pistachio Popsicle. She's also working on a Bloody Maria with a stalk of celery, but she doesn't offer him anything.

"Well, buster," she trumpets, "I've solved your case for you!"

"Oh?" he says. "And how have you managed that?"

She tells him how this guy came to her and offered to sell the eggs back for eight hundred thousand. She made a deal, and when she prepares a package of cut-up newspaper, the exchange will take place. McBryde can be there and grab the guy and the eggs at the same time.

"How do you like that?" she says triumphantly.

He looks at her steadily. "How many meets have you had with this man?"

"Two."

"Did he tell you his name?"

"He didn't have to. I know him. He's Sam Davidson, a skin-flick producer."

McBryde stands, puts his hands on his hips, glares at her.

"Oh-oh," she says, "I don't like that look."

"I've never called a woman a shithead," he says, "but I'm going to start now. You shithead! If you had a brain, you'd be dangerous."

"Hey, wait a minute," she protests. "That's my line."

"The last time I saw Sam Davidson I was digging him out of a closet where he was locked up with a couple of Chinese chippies."

"What?!"

"You heard me. It was in the Park Avenue apartment of the guy who copped your eggs from the last thief. If you had told me when Davidson first came to you, I could have picked him up, leaned on him, and the chances are good that you'd have your eggs back right now. But no, you had to take charge, do things your way, and fuck everything up royally.

Now Davidson is out of the picture, and a fake Hasidic Jew has the eggs. All because you had to prove what a hotshot detective you are."

"Well, screw you!" she says hotly. "You weren't getting anywhere, were you? Just futzing around with Yum-Yum decals and white Jaguars."

"When the hell are you going to get it through your tiny, tiny brain that I'm a professional cop, trained for this kind of work. You're a lousy civilian amateur, and just because you've got a scenic set of boobs, you figure you're a nuclear physicist. Will you just butt out and let me do my job?"

"You asshole!" she screams at him. "You think tits are the secret of my success? Think again, sonny boy. It's taken a lot of talent, hard work, and learning how to survive in this dog-eat-dog world."

"Oh, sure," he jeers. "Now tell me it's a jungle out there."

"Well, it is, you stupe! And a hundred times tougher for a woman than a man. But I don't expect a moron like you to understand that. Let me tell you something, kiddo—you keep farting around with your cockamamy clues, and I'm going to keep trying to get my eggs back by myself. You call yourself a professional cop? My God, you probably have to wait for a Boy Scout to cross the street."

"Up yours!" they sing out in unison.

Queens, NY

It's not yet noon, and they're sitting at a table in the steakhouse as the waiters bustle about, getting set up for lunch. Fat Wanda is drinking beer, but Rocco Castellano, Vito Zivic, and Morry are working on a big pot of coffee and a plate of toasted anise bread from Mama Lucia's bakery right down the street.

Morry is laughing so hard he can hardly finish his story. "So Shakespeare comes scrambling up Park Avenue, running as fast as he can, carrying the two jugs and trying to hang onto his crazy hat at the same time. And after him comes these two guys, a tall black and a little slant-eye—I guess they were the ones who lost the eggs—and they're both screaming like maniacs. And then, from across Park, this gang of cops comes rushing, blowing whistles and hauling out their irons. I was parked where I could see all the action, and I like to die laughing. I tell you it was a riot!"

"That Shakespeare," Rocco marvels. "What a cute shnorrer he is. He got away okay?"

"Oh, sure. He pops into the Cadillac he came in, and his driver takes off like a bat outta hell. I go after them, but everyone else is left standing on the sidewalk with their thumbs up their ass. Pardon my language, Wanda."

"I heard worse," she says, belching delicately.

"So I follow the Cadillac down Fifth," Morry continues. "Traffic is murder, so I don't have no trouble sticking on their tail. I even get close enough to see the actor taking off his Yiddish threads in the back seat. I figure they'll take the eggs back to Zucchi at the Bedlington, but no, they keep going down Fifth and then turn east to Gramercy Park. They stop outside a grungy little town house on East 20th Street. I got the address wrote down here. Shakespeare carries the eggs inside, and the Cadillac takes off. I hang around awhile, but the actor don't come out. I slipped a fin to the super next door, and he tells me the town house is owned by a loopy dame named Gwendolyn Farquhar. I got that wrote down, too. I stayed around till it got dark. Then, when it looked like Shakespeare was in for the night, I come home."

"You done real good, Morry," Castellano says approvingly. "Now you better go back to East 20th in case they decide to move the eggs. Wanda, you get back to the Bedlington and keep an eye on Zucchi. I want all bases covered on this one."

After they leave, Zivic says to his chief, "Lucky that Shakespeare didn't take the eggs to the hotel. It's a lot easier hitting a private place."

"Just what I was thinking," Castellano says, reading the scrawled note Morry has left him. "Maybe sometime today you and me will take a ride over there and case the joint. Like how many people live there, locks on the outside door, fire escapes, and so forth."

"How soon you want to hit it?" Vito asks.

"As soon as we can. Before they make a deal with Marilyn."

"After we get the eggs, you really going to ask for a million?"

"That's what I'll *ask*, but I'll settle for half. It'll be worth it just to give the shaft to The Man from Chicago. Can you imagine his nerve, muscling in on our turf? The guy's got to learn to play fair."

Manhattan, NY

Sergeant Rumfry hits it on his eighteenth phone call. This theatrical costumer on Tenth Avenue says yeah, he rented out a Hasidic outfit a few days ago. As a matter of fact, it was returned just that morning.

Rumfry and the lieutenant get over there in a hurry. McBryde talks to Dr. Frankenstein's monster while the sergeant takes notes.

"This guy who rented the Hasidic costume—did he say what he wanted it for? Theater? Masquerade party?"

"Nope," the monster says. "Just said he wanted something religious."

"You get his name and address?"

"Sure, I got it right here on the sales slip. Mario Zucchi. The Hotel Bedlington. That's over on Madison."

"I know where it is. What did this man look like?"

"Tall. Thin. He must have been a pretty boy once, but now he looks like he's done a lot of hard living. But still handsome."

"How old do you figure?"

"Oh, maybe pushing forty."

"What color hair?"

"Long, wavy black. Looked dyed."

"Eyes?"

"Washed-out blue."

"You're an observant man. Did he talk with an accent?"

"Phony English upper class. Actorish."

"You think he was a professional actor?"

"Could have been. A lousy one."

"Anything else unusual about him?"

"His clothes. The buttons on his jacket were glass eyes. I notice things like that."

"Yeah, I imagine you would."

"And he had a daisy pinned on his lapel."

"In other words, a real Fancy Dan."

"You got it."

"Thank you, monster. You've been a big help."

On their way over to the Bedlington, Rumfry says, "How do you want to handle it? Waltz in there and grab him?"

"No," McBryde says, "you stay in the car and let me go in alone and nose around first. It just doesn't make sense that a guy clever enough to pull a caper like that would use his own name. So it's either a complete phony or he's using someone else's."

"Someone staying at the hotel?"

"That's possible. Which might mean the actor is staying at the hotel, too."

The lieutenant saunters into the Bedlington, looks around, goes up to the desk. It takes a moment to catch the attention of the clerk, a twit with a mustache that looks as if it was drawn on his upper lip with an eyebrow pencil.

"I'm looking for Mr. Mario Zucchi," McBryde says. "He told me he'd be staying here."

"Mr. Zucchi is registered."

"Is he in?"

"No."

"Can you tell me when he'll be back?"

"He didn't say."

"May I leave a message?"

The clerk shrugs.

"Maybe I'll just hang around awhile. He might show up."

McBryde spots the sign, Cocktail Lounge, and goes in there. The place is empty except for the bartender who's reading a racing form.

"Any winners?" McBryde asks pleasantly.

"Winners?" the barman says bitterly. "What's that?"

"I'm looking for Mr. Zucchi. Has he been in?"

"Not today. Not yet he hasn't."

"Maybe he's at an audition."

"An audition? What for?"

"Well, the man *is* an actor."

The bartender stares at him. "I don't think we're talking about the same guy. Zucchi, the one staying at the hotel, is a businessman. Import-export."

"He's not tall, slender, good-looking? About forty? Sharp dresser?"

"Nah. He's like fifty-five. Built like a dumpster. A polyester type."

"Sorry," McBryde says, "I guess I got my wires crossed."

The lieutenant goes back outside, climbs into the car next to Rumfry. He tells the sergeant what he learned in the hotel.

"Something isn't kosher," he says fretfully. "The barkeep says Zucchi is a businessman in import-export. That's the oldest gag in the book and could cover everything from smuggling bearer bonds to white slavery. I think I'll hang around here, see if I can get any skinny from the bellhops. They know *everything*. You go back to the office and run Mario Zucchi through Records. Really do a job on him. Let's see if we can find out what Mr. Zucchi is importing and exporting."

"Could be eggs," the sergeant says.

"Could be," McBryde agrees.

Manhattan, NY

As Shakespeare mentioned, his ladyfriend on Gramercy Park is a woman of magnificent embonpoint. In addition, she has a delightful case of steatopygia so that in left silhouette she looks like a plump S. Crowning her monumental presence is a mobcap of frizzy curls, carroty in color.

Shakespeare, smoking a cigarette in a long holder of delft porcelain, watches as her nimble fingers embroider a portrait of Franklin Pierce. Eventually, the canvas will cover a presidential footstool, to be added to the thirteen already completed. Then, on to James Buchanan!

"You know, Gwen," the actor says, "the men I work for are really dreadful people."

"There are so many in the world," she says.

"True, but my employers are particularly distasteful. Lower drawer, all of them. Even a hint of culture is totally lacking. Yet, by force of circumstance, I am doomed to depend on them for my livelihood."

"All work is ennobling," she observes. "No matter how humble."

"I do assure you that my labors are far from humble. They are, in fact, enormously remunerative. But I am never allowed to share fully in the fruits of my efforts. I am what is vulgarly called a hired hand."

"I thought I might make veal cordon bleu tonight," she says brightly. "But veal is so expensive I plan to substitute liverwurst. Do you think that will work?"

"It's worth a try," he says bravely. "I don't wish to seem immodest, old girl, but I am infinitely more intelligent than the peasants who employ me. More talented. More imaginative. In addition, I take risks from which they profit mightily. It is not a happy situation."

"Or sliced salami," she says reflectively. "That might succeed."

"Possibly," Shakespeare says. "For instance, those two plastic flasks in the bathroom—I obtained them by careful planning and more than a soupçon of derring-do. They have the potential of a large, a *very* large profit that I shall never share. I recognize that life is frequently unfair, but this seems to me to border on rank injustice. It simply is not right."

She looks up at him. "If you could be a bird," she asks, "what kind would you like to be?"

"At the moment," he says, "a hawk. And you?"

"A robin redbreast."

"Charming," he said, then rises to his feet, suddenly resolute. "Gwen, I must make a call. I'll use the phone in the kitchen, if I may."

"Or perhaps a pileated sapsucker," she says thoughtfully.

He looks up the phone number of Marilyn Taylor Merchandise, Inc., in the directory and calls. Eventually he is connected to a man who identifies himself as Gary Flomm, Ms. Taylor's public relations aide. Using his Dr. Krankheit accent, Shakespeare states that he is in possession of Marilyn's eggs. Under questioning by Flomm, he describes the refrigerator flask accurately.

He then waits patiently and finally hears that famous voice.

"This is Taylor," she says crisply. "I understand you have my eggs. How much do you want?"

The actor explains that it is not a subject he wishes to discuss on the phone and suggests a personal meeting.

"All right," she says immediately. "You want to come here?"

"Oh, no," he says hastily. "I think the Central Park Zoo would be nice. The monkey house. Tomorrow at noon. Just the two of us. No policemen, please."

"I'll be there," she says. "And no cops. How will I know you from the monkeys?"

"I'll have a miniature orchid in my buttonhole."

"That should do it," she says, and hangs up.

Satisfied, Shakespeare returns to the living room and pours his hostess a glass of Thunderbird at the marble-topped sideboard.

"Gwen," he says, "how would you like to spend some time on the French Riviera?"

"How much time?"

"The rest of our lives," he says gaily.

Manhattan, NY

Mario Zucchi finally locates The Man from Chicago at his country club where the don is attending his nephew's wedding reception. Mario can hear sounds of raucous festivities in the background, punctuated by what seem to be gunshots but which The Man assures him are merely jumbo firecrackers.

"Glad to hear it," The Nose says. "I just wanted to report that Shakespeare got the merchandise."

"Excellent!" Chicago cries happily. "I knew he'd come through for us."

"Yeah," Zucchi says, "but there's a fly in the erntment. I figured he'd bring the stuff back to my room here at the hotel. But he took it down to a place on Gramercy Park where he's staying with some bimbo."

"Oh?" The Man says, and now his voice is cold and toneless. "Why did he do that?"

"He claims the merchandise would be safer there. He says if we kept it in the hotel, it might be spotted by a maid."

There is a moment's silence. Then: "I don't like it. There's big money involved here. I wouldn't like to think the actor is planning a cross."

"You think he'd pull that? After all we done for him? I figured he was a friend of ours."

The Man sighs. "Mario, when are you going to learn that when big bucks are up for grabs, there's no such things as friends. You know exactly where Shakespeare is staying?"

"Oh, sure. Dino's been down there. He's got the address."

"Good. Now what I want you to do is hit the place. Just walk in, grab the merchandise, and leave. Tell the actor you're following my orders. Take the stuff back to your hotel and hide it. You follow?"

"I got it. There are plenty of soldiers here. But we may have to rent another car for the hit."

"Then rent it. The next time you phone me I want to hear you have the merchandise in your possession."

"What about Shakespeare? You want we should bounce him around a little, to show him who's boss?"

"No, that won't be necessary," The Man says. "Just tell him to return to Chicago. I'll take care of him."

Manhattan, NY

McBryde tells Gripsholm how he traced the Hasidic getup to Mario Zucchi at the Hotel Bedlington.

"But he doesn't match the description of the guy who lifted the eggs from the Park Avenue apartment. So I ran a check on this Zucchi. He's a Mafia boss from LA. Into drugs, extortion, porn films—you name it. So, with an okay from the hotel, I put in an undercover bellhop. He searched Zucchi's suite and the rooms of the soldiers he's got with him, and came up with zilch. He swears Marilyn's eggs aren't in the hotel."

"Then where the hell are they?"

"I think the guy who swiped them, the actor, is holding them. I'm betting he's working for the mob. So I've put a twenty-four-hour shadow on Zucchi, figuring that sooner or later he's going to make contact. Then, with luck, we can tail Zucchi to the eggs."

"But you've got no proof that Zucchi and the actor are in cahoots."

"That's right; no proof. But I can't believe an LA mobster came to New York just to visit the ballet and Frick Museum. Zucchi has a long sheet, including robbery and felonious assault. And he did a year in a federal pokey for income tax fraud. The guys in the Organized Crime Bureau tell me the LA mob is controlled from Chicago. So this is a high-level operation. I figure that now that they've got the eggs, Marilyn Taylor will be hearing from them soon. I'm going back to my office and phone her. Maybe we can set up a trap at the payoff."

"If someone else doesn't swipe the eggs first," Gripsholm says gloomily.

The lieutenant returns to his office and considers how he should handle this call, remembering their last conversation was pure *Sturm und Drang*. He decides his best course is to be official, terse, even icy. But when he hears her voice, his stern resolve melts away.

"I just want to apologize," he says huskily. "I acted like—"

"Oh, shut up," she says. "When the time is right, I'll match you crawl for crawl. But right now we've got other fish to fry. Be at the monkey house in the Central Park Zoo tomorrow at noon."

"What?" he says. "What the hell are you talking about?"

She tells him.

Manhattan, NY

Shakespeare borrows Gwendolyn's old, pot-bellied Buick and drives up to Central Park. He saunters casually about the zoo, the debonair boulevardier in his rakish fedora. But his pale eyes are busy enough, searching for signs of a police presence. He sees nothing untoward and strolls to the rendezvous.

Marilyn Taylor is wearing her black wig, no hat, a scrubby trench coat, and dark sunglasses. She stands planted before a tribe of cavorting monkeys, hoping none of them will ask for an autograph. Suddenly she feels her long tresses lifted.

"Come out, come out, whoever you are," a man sings lightly.

She turns slowly and sees the miniature orchid pinned to Shakespeare's lapel.

"What happened to the accent?" she asks.

"I'm doing Noel Coward today, dearie," he says.

She gets a good look at him. "I know you," she says. "Loring Minchley Flotsom. I caught you in LA the night you bombed in *Hamlet.*"

"You and a million others," he says, sighing. "Or so it seems."

"Then you disappeared. Gave up the theater and took up crime, did you?"

"Not quite," he says, and she must admit his smile is charming. Raddled, but charming. "I just decided to extend my range. Make a performance of my entire life."

"And now you're playing a thief?"

"Exactly."

"You want to stand here or walk around?"

"Let's stay right here." He glances about. "Didn't bring any friends along, I hope."

"You should know better than that. I want my eggs back and wouldn't do anything to queer the deal. You really have them?"

"I really have them. Just call me Eggs Diamond."

"Very funny. How much do you want?"

"Half a million. Cash."

There is silence. They both stare at a young chimpanzee sitting placidly on a rock, abusing himself.

"Doesn't he realize he may go blind?" Shakespeare asks.

She laughs. "You're totally insane. And a half a million is also totally insane. It's a lot of money."

"For me, not for you."

"That's what everyone thinks," she says angrily. "But I assure you I don't consider half a million just petty cash."

"But you want your eggs."

"Yes, I want my eggs."

"Well," he says, shrugging, "the ball is in your court, old girl. I think haggling is dreadfully demeaning, don't you. So half a mil it is. The decision is yours."

"How much time do I have?"

"To make up your mind? Twenty-four hours. I'll call you tomorrow, noonish. If it's yes, we'll arrange another meeting to work out the details."

"And if it's no?"

"Then I'm afraid your eggs will end up in a New Jersey landfill."

"Have you no compassion?" she cries.

"Great line," he says. "You used it in *Beer and Bustles,* didn't you?"

"I may have," she acknowledges. "I've made a lot of films, played a lot of roles, delivered a lot of lines. Sometimes they intrude on reality."

"My point exactly, dear lady," he says. "One reason I decided to *live* as an actor."

She looks at him curiously. "But do you know who *you* are?"

He shakes his head. "Don't know and couldn't care less."

"Seems to me I heard you were a hophead, and that's why you screwed up *Hamlet.* Is that true?"

He grins elfishly. "And I heard you ball everyone on the set, including grips and gofers. Is that true?"

She laughs. "Look, call me tomorrow about the eggs."

"Will do," he says. "But before we part I must tell you how much I admire your talent. I wish we could have worked together."

"We are," she says. "Now."

"True," he agrees, and lifts a languid hand in farewell.

She waits another five minutes, as instructed, watching the scampering simians but not seeing them. Then she moves to the polar bears. McBryde meets her there.

"You okay?" he asks anxiously.

"I just gave the greatest performance of my career, but I admit I'm a mite spooked."

"Why? Did he come on heavy?"

"Oh, no. But I recognized him. Loring Minchley Flotsom. He used to be on the stage."

"Was he any good?"

"He could have been. But the talk was that he had started snorting. He murdered Hamlet's soliloquy one night, and that finished him."

"A duster? Well, you had nothing to worry about; you were covered."

"I was? How?"

"Didn't you notice that young couple with the kid who were standing near you? The man was Officer Sol Applebaum. The woman was Officer Sally Crumble. She works in Inspector Gripsholm's office and was happy to get out from behind a desk."

"Don't tell me that kid was an undercover cop, too."

"No, he belongs to Sergeant Rumfry. His mother was delighted to get him out of the house for a day."

"Listen, McBryde, with all those cops around, why didn't you nab Flotsom right then and there?"

"You want your eggs back, don't you? The actor is going to lead us to them. I've got two men tailing him, and two cars standing by."

"All right," she says, "you're the director. Can we go now?"

"Sure. Give you a lift home?"

On the ride back to her town house, she turns sideways so she can look at him.

"How do you like me with black hair?" she asks.

"Dynamite," he says. "Jezebel."

"But you don't like it?"

"Not much."

"Okay," she says, taking off the wig and dark sunglasses. "How's that?"

"Much better. Now your collar and cuffs match."

She laughs and punches his arm. "If you find my eggs and arrest Flotsom, what'll happen to him?"

"That's a tough one. He stole the eggs—but from another thief, Champ DuBois. And *he* lifted them from another thief, Ronald Yates, who swiped them from the original thief, Nicholas Kazanian. I guess we could rack them all up for receiving stolen property, if you want to press charges."

"But you don't think I should?"

"It's up to you. You've got a lot of clout; you know that. You can make it as hard or as easy on those people as you want."

She ponders a moment. "I'd hate to see Flotsom behind bars," she says finally. "I really feel sorry for the guy."

"That's what I figured. Why don't you wait until you get your eggs back, and then we'll sort it out."

"Whatever you say, boss."

They pull up in front of her town house, and McBryde kills the engine. "Can we talk a minute?"

"About what?"

"You and me. I started to apologize yesterday. Now let me finish. I'm sorry I blew my stack and called you names. But I was so goddamned frustrated by this case, and your meeting with Sam Davidson without telling me was the last straw."

"It was a stupid thing to do," she agrees. "You had every right to be sore. It's just that I've gotten so used to running everything and everybody that I thought I could manage this, too. Okay, now that we've both crawled, are we still pals?"

"I hope so."

"You should smile more often," she says. "Your whole face lights up. Usually you're a sourpuss. Tell me something, McBryde: You like being a cop?"

"Of course I like it. It's the only job I've ever had and the only one I want."

"But you don't make much of a salary, do you?"

"I get by."

"I've got this huge, complex organization, and it's getting too much for me to handle. I need someone I can trust. How's about moving out to the left coast and learning the business. My business."

"Thanks, but no, thanks."

"I could start you off at twice what you're making now."

"And what would my title be—Stud-in-Residence? Look, I appreciate the offer, but it's got nothing to do with what I want."

"Which is?"

"Being a cop, a good cop. Getting married. Eventually."

"And the patter of tiny feet?"

"Sure, that's part of it."

"Sounds to me like you've got your life all planned."

"Come on, give me a break! You asked me what I wanted, and I told you. You don't *plan* meeting someone you want to marry. You don't *plan* having kids. You hope. Now you know what I hope for. What do you hope for?"

"Right now? I hope you'll leave this clunker double-parked, come upstairs, and do a little Romeo-and-Julieting."

"I'll have to call the office first."

"You would," she says. "My demon lover."

Boston, MA

"I do believe," says Monsignor O'Dell, "that we are proceeding as rationally and expeditiously as circumstances warrant."

"I concur," says Professor T. Hiram Farthingale.

Warmed by self-satisfaction, they squirm their ecclesiastic and judicial butts deeper into the leather chairs and lift brandy snifters to their schnozzes to inhale the fumes.

"I have received a second letter from Rome," O'Dell reports. "I think that's encouraging since it indicates continuing interest in our project."

"Excellent," the professor says. "For my part, I have hinted to my FBI friends that a plan is under consideration by high authorities that would grant them a key role in the investigation. They are, of course, enormously pleased and promise their wholehearted cooperation. So I believe we may safely conclude that matters are progressing in superlative fashion. Would you care for a cigar, Terry?"

"I would indeed, thank you."

They light up and puff away blissfully.

"You know, old friend," the monsignor says thoughtfully, "the theft of Marilyn's eggs has provided us with many hours of invigorating debate. But I believe it has had an additional salubrious effect."

"Oh? And what may that be?"

"Why, Hiram, it has, in a sense, energized us, has it not? We are both in the autumn of our years—if not early winter—and yet this dastardly crime has stirred us to action."

"It is of some personal gratification," Farthingale admits. "I am sure you felt, as I did, that our days as movers and shakers were lost in the limbo of time. And yet we have reacted to this heinous affront to civilized mores like old firehouse horses. We have heard the alarm, and we have come charging, eyes aglitter and nostrils flaring."

"Is it not remarkable, old friend, that our—dare I use the word *renaissance;* perhaps *revival* would be more fitting—was activated by a criminal conspiracy against a woman who is a complete stranger to us."

There is silence for a moment.

"Not quite a *complete* stranger," the professor says hesitatingly. "I must confess, Terry, that I have seen all of Marilyn's movies. And enjoyed them greatly, I might add."

"And I," O'Dell says dreamily, "must also confess. I have in my wallet, many times unfolded and folded, a photograph of Marilyn that appeared in a newspaper several years ago. She is wearing a rather abbreviated bathing costume of her own design."

"I know that picture well!" Farthingale says excitedly. "Two Stamps and a Band-Aid!"

"Hotsy-totsy!" the monsignor says, beaming.

Manhattan, NY

"Two cars should be enough," Mario Zucchi tells his assembled soldiers. "I'll boss one, Dino the other." He checks the magazine of his 7.65mm Beretta. "Keep your irons out, but no bang-bang if we can avoid it. The hardware's just for show. There's only Shakespeare and his dolly, so I'm not expecting no trouble."

"What if he won't let us in?" Dino asks.

"Whaddya think? We bust down the door. The big thing is to get in quick, grab the eggs, and get out fast. Then we come back here, and I call Chicago. Now let's all have a belt. We'll get there at midnight."

Queens, NY

"Two cars should be enough," Rocco Castellano tells Vito Zivic. "You take one with three guys, and I'll take the other with Morry." He checks the action on his 9mm Luger. "No rough stuff unless we have to. There's just Shakespeare and his woman, so there shouldn't be no hassle."

"But if there is?" Zivic asks.

Castellano shrugs. "Then we handle it. Figure to be on East 20th Street at midnight. We go in fast, take the eggs, and get out in a hurry. Then we come back here and celebrate."

"What if the actor comes on strong?"

"Don't worry it," Rocco advises. "Believe me, it'll go like silk."

Manhattan, NY

"Two cars should be enough," Lieutenant McBryde tells Sergeant Rumfry. "You take one, I'll take the other." He loads his .38 service revolver. "According to the men who tailed Flotsom, there's just him and a woman in the town house, so I don't anticipate any problems."

"We collar both of them?" Rumfry asks.

"Of course. But we don't leave without the egg flask and the container of extra liquid nitrogen. That's very important."

"What time do you want to make it?"

"Let's say midnight. There shouldn't be many people around at that hour."

Manhattan, NY

"They have topless beaches on the French Riviera, luv," Shakespeare teases. "You might really become a robin redbreast."

"May I take my knitting?" Gwendolyn asks.

"Of course you may."

"Loring," she says, comparing her embroidered canvas with an etching of Franklin Pierce, "you're doing something illegal, aren't you?"

"Somewhat," he says airily. "But I assure you that no one will suffer from my illicit activities."

"If you're arrested, will we go to jail?"

"If we do," he says, "I'll insist on adjoining cells. But the chances— Oh, drat! Someone's at the door. Don't bestir yourself, old girl; I'll get it."

He opens the outside door carelessly.

"Hullo, Shakespeare," Zucchi says, not smiling.

"Why, Mario, what a pleasant surprise! Out for a midnight jaunt, are you?"

"Not exactly," The Nose says. "Chicago wants me to hold the eggs. So just hand them over, and I'll be on my way."

"Love to, old man, but I don't have them. I moved the swag to a more secure location, y'see."

"Uh-huh. Okay, boys, toss the place."

Zucchi forces the door wide and enters. After him come crowding his band of ruffians. Gwendolyn Farquhar looks up as the mob surges into her living room.

"Guests!" she says brightly. "How nice! Perhaps I'll put water on for a pot of oolong."

"Don't bother, ma'am," Zucchi says politely. "We're not staying."

He motions, and his men fan out through the town house. He remains in the living room, watching Shakespeare. The actor leans negligently against the mantel, fitting a cigarette to his porcelain holder.

"Putting on a little weight, aren't you, Mario?" he asks. "You look a bit puffy about the gills."

Before Zucchi can reply, Dino comes back into the living room lugging the two refrigerator containers.

"Got 'em," he reports to his boss. "They was in the terlet."

Mario stares coldly at the actor. "You really were figuring a cross, weren't you? The Man wants you back in Chicago right away. He'll take care of you. Dino, give me the jugs. You round up the guys, and we'll get out of here."

Zucchi's gang reassembles and moves to the outside door.

"Sorry you couldn't stay," Gwendolyn calls after them. "Do drop by again."

Dino opens the door, and Rocco Castellano steps in.

"And I didn't even have to knock," he says. "Hiya, Mario. Can we join the party?"

He bulls his way forward, followed by his henchmen. Zucchi, still gripping the flasks, backs into the living room, surrounded by his gang.

"So you did come back," Gwendolyn says happily. "And you brought some friends. Goodness, I'm afraid I don't have enough chairs."

Zucchi puts down the jugs. "I'm going out of here, Rocco," he says. "With the eggs."

"Over my dead body," Castellano says.

"That can be arranged," Mario says, pulling out his Beretta.

Rocco swats the gun aside and grapples with Zucchi. A melee erupts. With shouts, curses, cries of triumph, and yelps of pain, blows are struck, arms twisted, men are tripped and go thundering down. Shakespeare takes Gwendolyn by the arm and tugs her away from the imbroglio. They stand against the wall, watching the carnage.

The battle rages over the living room with chairs and tables overturned, lamps going down with a crash, the presidential footstools wielded as clubs. The claret flows, and bloodied men stagger to their feet to trade wild punches, and then resort to gouging, hacking, and angry kicks.

"Freeze!" shouts Lieutenant Jeffrey McBryde as he enters, gripping his service revolver. "Will you all, for God's sake, freeze!"

No one freezes. If anything, the brannigan intensifies, and McBryde, Rumfry, and the uniformed officers go wading into the welter of flailing mobsters. The cops try to separate the combatants, using their saps to bring peace. But the turmoil continues.

In the midst of this chaos, Shakespeare picks up the two plastic flasks, and he and Gwendolyn begin sidling toward the outside door, dodging flying footstools, stepping over fallen bodies, and ducking to avoid the swings of the cops' truncheons.

They are quietly exiting, almost tiptoeing, when Mario Zucchi, nose battered and bleeding, spots their retreat.

"Feci!" he screams. "The sonofabitch is stealing my eggs!"

Then everyone freezes. They turn to see the actor and his companion leave the town house, Shakespeare carrying the jugs. Immediately there is a frantic rush into the hallway, but so many are trying to get to the outside door that the crowd jams, men struggle, mouth horrible oaths, claw at those ahead, and, in turn, are clawed by those behind.

Eventually, villains and policemen alike debouch onto 20th Street in time to see a fat black Buick pull away from the curb. There are furious yells, roars, howls, and they all dash madly for their cars. Engines whine, tires squeal as gangster and cop cars race in pursuit.

The chase heads up First Avenue, horns blaring, sirens wailing. Zucchi's cars, Castellano's, and McBryde's are intermixed, higgledy-piggledy, with drivers hunched over their wheels, paying no attention to traffic signals and pushing their heaps as if they were at Le Mans.

"View halloo!" carols Shakespeare, tooling the fat Buick with delighted abandon. "The hunt is on, and we're the sly fox. Isn't this *fun,* old girl!"

"I do hope someone remembered to lock the front door," Gwendolyn says, hanging on as they swerve to avoid slower vehicles and career around corners.

The actor drives a zigzag course, heading northward and turning west when traffic jams up ahead of him. Strung out in his wake come the mobsters and New York's Finest, all smashing speed limits as they jockey for position.

No one knows who fires the first shot, but after that a fusillade erupts, rapid, continuous, and mercifully inaccurate. On 25th Street a bullet penetrates the plate-glass window of the Gimme-Gimme Boutique, decapitating a mannequin wearing lounging pajamas made of gunnysacks.

Lieutenant McBryde, in the leading police car, works his radio feverishly, calling in squads from all over Manhattan and giving the dispatcher a running update of their position. When the gunfire begins, he unholsters his revolver and plinks at the tires of Zucchi's Cadillac ahead of him.

The cavalcade hurtles on, across 28th to Third Avenue, up Third to 35th, westward to Park Avenue and then northward again. It is on 35th Street that a bullet pierces the window of the Filthy Shame Bar & Grill. It strikes and shatters a bottle of Pizzle Beer being imbibed by an habitué who is so shaken by the incident that he immediately swears off strong drink, a vow respected for at least eight minutes.

Shakespeare leads the chase over to Madison Avenue and continues his reckless course northward. By this time three more police cars have joined the parade, and there is no slackening of gunfire as pedestrians dive into doorways and uninvolved cars drive up on sidewalks to escape the oncoming juggernaut.

At 53rd Street a car occupied by newlyweds, Mr. and Mrs. Launcelot Becque, of Quebec, turns onto Madison and is locked into the tumultuous procession.

"It's TV, hon!" Mr. Becque says gleefully, speeding up. "They're doing a show, and we're right in the middle of it! Wait'll the folks back home hear about this!"

The cars race up Madison, the actor keeping ahead of his pursuers with demented driving that scatters dog walkers, joggers, crack dealers, and a bevy of elegantly dressed ladies and gentlemen who have just left a bar mitzvah at The Plaza.

The Buick enters Central Park at 59th Street and charges up the East Drive, scaring the bejesus out of the horse and driver of a barouche, but inspiring the passengers, four Japanese tourists sozzled on sake, to cry out, "Banzai, mothelfuckel!"

Hearing the whine of sirens approaching from all directions, Shakespeare turns left against traffic after crossing Traverse No. 1. Then, seeing the flashing red light bars of police cars coming closer, he bumps over the curb and takes off across country. The Buick twists around trees, crashes through bushes and shrubs, and eventually emerges onto Sheep Meadow. And right behind come the police, enraged mobsters, and Mr. and Mrs. Launcelot Becque.

"Tally-ho!" the actor sings out. "Gone to ground!"

He begins swinging around the Meadow in wide circles. As more police squads arrive, the spiral contracts until the entire cortege is tightly wound up. Fenders scrape, bumpers bend, glass shatters, and finally the chase comes to a screeching halt.

Cops come spilling out, weapons brandished.

"Bust everyone!" McBryde bellows.

The World

New York *News:*   EGG HEIST CRACKED!

New York *Post:*   EGGS BACK! "Well done!" says star.

New York *Newsday:*   EGG MYSTERY ALL OVA!

New York *Times:*   Stolen Eggs Recovered by Police in
                             Midnight Chase that Terrifies Many

The recovery of Marilyn Taylor's eggs immediately arouses universal excitement that surpasses the sensation caused by their theft. Newspapers, television, and radio bring the good news to the world's nations, and there is a great outpouring of joy and thanksgiving.

The actress, in a televised news conference, tearfully thanks everyone for their concern and prayers. She lauds the efforts of the New York Police Department, and singles out Lieutenant Jeffrey McBryde for his "brilliant detective work" that eventually led to the solution of the crime.

Once again her office is deluged with cablegrams, letters, and phone calls, but now they are all congratulatory. Included in this flood of messages is a warm note from the First Family and a copy of a resolution passed by both Houses of Congress expressing happiness at the recovery of her eggs and admiration for the brave manner with which she endured their temporary loss. Leaders of several countries, including the People's Republic of China and Swaziland, also send their best wishes.

To celebrate the felicitous outcome of the case, the Mayor of New York proclaims Marilyn Taylor Day, and all city workers are given a half day off. An outdoor ceremony is held at City Hall during which Marilyn is given a key to the city and a scroll. The occasion is somewhat marred by the throwing of eggs at the assembled dignitaries. The miscreants are later identified as members of a left-wing group seeking to have free condoms distributed at banks and subway change booths.

Celebrations are held elsewhere in the world, including one in a Glasgow, Scotland, soccer stadium. A riot results, and several celebrants are injured by flying haggis. Similarly, a street festival in Dijon, France, is spoiled when it is discovered that local Communists have torn down all the life-size posters of Marilyn affixed to pissoirs and replaced them with photographs of Mrs. Gorbachev.

But those are the unfortunate exceptions. In other places the mood is one of unrestrained joy. For instance, in Waco, Texas, what is claimed to be the World's Largest Barbecue is held in Marilyn's honor, necessitating the slaughter of 3,000 hogs. And in Cremona, Italy, the World's Largest Pizza is baked to celebrate the recovery of Marilyn's eggs. This giant pie requires the purchase of 867 bushels of tomatoes, 1,026 pounds of mozzarella, four kilometers of pepperoni, and a half ton of bicarbonate of soda.

From Moscow, *Izvestia* reports there is dancing in the streets of Pinsk.

Manhattan, NY

Guarded by Sergeant Rumfry and two uniformed officers, McBryde returns the refrigerator flasks to the East 63rd Street town house and proudly displays them to Marilyn Taylor and her exuberant staff.

"There they are," the lieutenant says. "That's what all the shooting was about. I checked them out, and the jug is safely topped off with liquid nitrogen."

"How can I ever thank you," Marilyn says.

"He'll think of a way," Harriet Boltz says, and her boss glares at her.

"But we better get them to Doc Primster as soon as possible," McBryde continues. "He's the only one who can tell if the eggs are still good. If it's okay with you, I'll have the sergeant take them over to the fertility clinic right now."

"You do that," Marilyn says. "Tell Primster I'll call him later today. McBryde, you come into my office; we've got business to discuss."

When they're alone, door closed, she gives him a tight hug and a big smooch.

"Thanks, kiddo," she says huskily.

"Thank *you* for the nice plug you gave the Department and me at your news conference."

"Well, you did a helluva job, and I appreciate it. You coulda got your ass shot off."

"Not really," he says. "There was a lot of noise, but everyone's aim was lousy—thank God."

"Where are all the bums now?"

"Out on bail. Except for a honeymooning couple from Canada. They got caught up in the case by accident. They thought someone was filming a TV thriller. When they learned those were real guns and real bullets, they almost fainted. They're back in Quebec now, telling all their friends that the Wild West is alive and well in New York."

"What's going to happen to the black hats?"

"I wanted to talk to you about that. We've got a sheet of charges as long as your arm. Disturbing the peace. Discharging a firearm. Breaking speed limits. Ignoring traffic signals. Reckless endangerment of pedestrians. Receiving stolen property. And on and on."

She stares at him. "But you don't want to go to trial?"

He sighs. "I had a long confab with Inspector Gripsholm and some of the Department's legal eagles. They agree we might nail the Mafia types on some minor charges, but putting them in the clink is very iffy. The actor is the only one who actually had possession of the eggs, and he took them from a previous thief. A smart lawyer could easily spring him. Plus, trying all those clowns would cost the City a mint. We've already spent a small fortune getting your eggs back."

"So you want the yobbos to walk?"

The lieutenant nods. "Let them plea-bargain the charges down to fines and probation. But all this is contingent on your okay. If you want to play hardball and stir up a ruckus in the press, then we'll have to go along."

She thinks a moment. "Nah," she says finally, "let's do it your way. I got my eggs back; that's all that matters. I have no interest in punishing a bunch of wetbrains."

"I was hoping you'd say that," the detective says. "You have no idea how much paperwork it's going to save me."

"All right," she says, "now we're finished with business—right? How about our own private celebration? Upstairs."

"Oh, yes," he says.

In her flouncy bedroom she skins down in a trice and then watches, with wonder, as he slowly and methodically undresses, shaking the wrinkles from his three-piece suit as he carefully folds and hangs it from a chairback.

Two hours later, she rests her head on his chest and says softly, "Did anyone ever tell you that you're habit-forming?"

"You're rather addictive yourself," he says gruffly.

"Well?" she demands. "What are we going to do about it?"

He doesn't reply.

"I've been thinking about what you said. You know, about how you want to stay a cop and get married and have a kid."

"And?"

"How about this: You keep your job and stay here. I'll move as much of my operation as I can to New York. But I'll still have to spend a lot of time in LA. We'll have a bicoastal marriage."

"Marriage?" he says, startled. "Are you proposing to me?"

"You've got it, buster. How about it?"

He moves from her gently, props himself on an elbow, stares down at her. "Seems to me no one's said anything about love."

"The L word?" she says with a honkish laugh. "I've said it so many times in so many films that it's lost its meaning."

"Not to me it hasn't. Want me to go first?"

"Yes. Cue me in."

"I love you," he says.

"And I love you," she says, trying to move closer to him. But he holds her away.

"All right," he says, "assuming we marry, what about kids?"

She sits up in bed, clasps her knees. "I've got to level with you, Mc-Bryde; I can't have kids."

"Why not?"

"At the same time I donated my eggs I had myself sterilized. Tubal ligation."

"Oh, Jesus. Why did you do that?"

"I was scared."

"Of what? Childbirth?"

"Come on, I've got enough gumption for that."

"Don't tell me again that you were afraid of losing your independence. I don't buy that."

"It's pure selfishness. And if you want to call it greed, that's okay. Look, McBryde, right now I've got the world by the nuts. I'm every man's wet dream, and most of the women like me, too. They envy my income and life-style: an important part of my public image. And I milk that image for every cent I can get, knowing it can't last forever. I'll get old, the public will get bored with me, some younger tootsie with bigger jugs and more teeth will come along and wipe me out. But right now I'm queen of the hill, and I'm cleaning up. But what if I have a kid?"

"Now I've got to level with you," he says. "I think you're full of crap. There's no proof that having a child would affect your career at all."

"No proof," she agrees, "but the danger is there. I've worked too hard and paid too many dues to run the risk of ruining everything by popping a tot. So I had myself fixed. Listen, if we got hitched, would you spring for adoption?"

"No," he says. "I want my own."

She takes a deep breath. "I was afraid you'd say that."

Neither speaks for a while. Then he gets out of bed and begins dressing.

"I guess that's it," he says stonily.

"Come here a minute," she says. "Don't run out on me."

He sits on the edge of the bed in his boxer shorts. She takes up his hand, presses knuckles to her cheek.

"There's a possibility," she says, "just a possibility, that the tubal ligation can be reversed. But it's tricky. No guarantees."

He withdraws his hand, strokes her cheek with fingertips.

"You'd do that for me?" he asks wonderingly.

"I don't like the idea of going under the knife, but I'll do it if it's the only way I can hang onto you. When I want something, or someone, I go after it no matter what."

"I guess you do."

"I'll have a talk with Primster and find out what the odds are of reversal being a success. You stand by until I find out. Don't go dipping your wick with anyone else."

"Not a chance," he says. "You've spoiled other women for me. You're the only one I want."

"Who writes your dialogue?" she says. "It sings! Now take off those bloomers and let's do a sequel."

Boston, MA

Monsignor O'Dell exits from Saint Bartholomew's Hermitage, tips his homburg to the moon, and begins his walk to Beacon Hill. But his step is draggy and his mien melancholic.

"Good evening, fayther," the housekeeper says, opening the door wide for him.

"Good evening, Bridget. And how is your rheumatism this evening?"

"Worse," she says shortly. "The Lord giveth and the Lord taketh away."

"Does He not," O'Dell says, sighing deeply.

Upstairs in the den, a silent Professor Farthingale, clad in a molting velvet dressing gown, greets his guest by proffering a snifter of cognac. Wordlessly the two oldsters slump disconsolately in their club chairs and regard each other with saddened eyes.

"I am, of course," the professor says finally, "absolutely delighted that Marilyn's eggs were recovered."

"I share your happiness," the monsignor says dolefully. "A joyous ending to a most unfortunate incident."

"But I would be less than honest," the host continues, "if I did not admit to a certain disappointment that our grand design was not destined to come to fruition."

"Perhaps a cigar may help alleviate our distress."

"Excellent suggestion."

They light up, sip their brandies, and gradually their mood levitates.

"Having expectations dashed is not a novel experience for me," Farthingale observes. "And, I would venture to say, in your lifetime you have had high hopes occasionally brought low."

"More than once," O'Dell agrees. "There was a time when I thought a cardinalship was within my grasp, but it was not to be. And I survived."

"And I once anticipated a federal judgeship, but it never materialized. Still, I am content with the path my life followed."

They sit in relaxed and comfortable silence a few moments, puffing their cigars, enjoying their cognac, ruminating on the drama that recently engaged their energies.

"Terry," the professor says after a while, "during the past few weeks, our aim was the eventual recovery of Marilyn's eggs, was it not?"

"That was certainly the spur to all our efforts."

"In which you cooperated fully. But those eggs were donated with the intention of making them available to a married friend of Marilyn's, to be fertilized *in vitro* by sperm from the friend's husband, and the resulting embryo to be implanted in the wife's uterus."

The monsignor straightens in his chair, sensing the opening moves in a merry wrangle that might keep them profitably employed for many pleasant evenings to come. He pours more brandy.

"And yet," the professor goes on, "that new technique of conception is expressly forbidden by your church. It is a contradiction that puzzles me: your efforts to help recover Marilyn's eggs despite the strictures of Rome."

O'Dell nods solemnly. "At first glance there may appear to be a dichotomy. But I believe closer examination will prove that my actions were completely in accord with papal homilies on the subject. What is important, Hiram, is to analyze, understand, and appreciate the motives involved: Marilyn's, in donating her eggs, and mine, in seeking their recovery."

And then away they go, reinvigorated by contention. Fresh cigars are lighted, cognac flows, and their intellectual shenanigans continue till the wee hours. Even then, the fervent debate is not concluded but merely postponed to another evening when they can prove once again that neither suffers from sclerosis of the bean and that logorrhea as an art form has not perished in Boston.

Manhattan, NY

"We bring you glad tidings," Dr. Reginald Primster says with his chilly smile. "Your eggs appear to be in tip-top condition."

"Wonderful! All nine of them?"

"Apparently so. We have taken the liberty of informing Mr. and Mrs. Bannon."

"I know," Marilyn says, "I talked to them. They're acting like kids on the night before Christmas. Eric says he has an appointment tomorrow to go into your Masturbatorium and do his duty."

Primster shows his big teeth. "We have found that the most cost-effective method of obtaining semen."

"Uh-huh. Tell me something, doc: How many of my eggs are you planning to use?"

"We usually transfer three embryos to the donee. That appears to be the optimum amount. Transferring more does not seem to have any effect on the rate of pregnancy, although it may increase the possibility of multiple pregnancies."

"I don't think Eve has any great desire to have quintuplets. Do you mind if I smoke?"

"Yes," he says, "we do."

Marilyn sighs. "It's getting so I have to go into a closet to light up. Now tell me something else: If you only use three of my eggs out of the nine, what happens to the rest?"

He shrugs. "That's up to you. They are your property."

"I had this wild idea . . . When those nudnicks were trying to hold me up for ransom on the eggs, they were asking about a hundred thousand dollars per egg. Are they worth that much?"

Primster stirs uncomfortably. "Exceedingly doubtful. It is true that on occasion women have been paid for donating their eggs to another woman. But we have never heard of a price in excess of one thousand dollars. Why do you ask?"

"I told you it was a wild idea. The New York Police Department spent a lot of money getting my eggs back, and I'd like to repay them. I was wondering if I could get Sotheby's or Christie's to auction off the remaining eggs, the proceeds to go to the NYPD. What do you think? Totally crazy?"

The doctor gapes in astonishment, then permits himself a frigid smile. "After the incredible events of the past several weeks we are not prepared to say that any action you may take in regard to your excess eggs is totally crazy. It would certainly be a novel way of helping solve the problem of infertility. As well as the budget problems of the police department."

"Yeah," Marilyn says thoughtfully, "and the publicity fallout would be tremendous. A real media event. I might get bids from all over the world."

"You might indeed."

"Well, I'll talk to my public relations people about it. But now I've got something more important to ask you: What are the chances of having my tubal ligation reversed?"

Primster stares at her a moment, shocked. "So soon? If you recall, we tried to dissuade you from sterilization, but you were adamant."

"I know, I know; I'm not blaming you. Just tell me if it can be reversed."

"Possibly. That's the most we can say. There can be no guarantees, ever, when surgery is involved. And reversal would require very difficult microsurgery. Would you mind telling us why you now desire reversal."

"I've met this guy I want to marry. That's fine with him, but he wants a child. His own; no adoption."

"And you're willing to endure surgery for his sake?"

"Yes."

For the first time Dr. Primster's smile is almost warm. "Surgery will not be necessary," he says.

"No surgery? But I can have a kid anyway?"

The doctor nods.

"How?" she says excitedly. "Tell me how!"

He tells her.

Cairo, Egypt

Ptolemy watches as Youssef Khalidi tucks into a luncheon of grilled ram testicles and figs.

"I'm being transferred," the CIA man says gloomily.

"Oh?"

"To Reykjavik."

"Ah. In Rumania?"

"Iceland."

Khalidi looks up from his food. "It is sometimes cold in Iceland?"

"Sometimes. They've made me the fall guy for Operation Soufflé, so they're shipping me out. We had units of the Sixth Fleet standing by, attack choppers on line, and fifty John Waynes all juiced up and hot to trot. Then they recover Marilyn's eggs in Central Park. I'm lucky Control didn't offer me a blindfold and a final cigarette."

Youssef finishes his meal, wipes his mouth on his sleeve. He lights up his narghile, blowing a plume of rancid smoke over Ptolemy's head. The agent leans across the table.

"Joe," he says, "you played me for a Yankee Doodle shvontz. Marilyn's eggs were never smuggled out of the country; they never left New York. There is no terrorist sect called Arm of God. There is no informer named Akmed. There is no mountain called Camel's Hump. It was all a scam—right?"

Khalidi nods sadly.

"Why did you do it?" Ptolemy asks indignantly. "My career is ruined. I'm the laughingstock of the Company. And now I've got to freeze my balls off in Iceland."

"All things are as Allah wills."

"Allah had nothing to do with it. *You* conned me. I figure you took Uncle Samuel for about ten grand American over the past few weeks. Why, Joe? *Why?*"

"My grandmother," Youssef says.

"Your grandmother? What has she got to do with it?"

"She needs orthodontic work."

Ptolemy leans back and stares at the dance floor. A lachrymose belly dancer is undulating to the strains of "Oh! How She Could Yacki, Hacki, Wicki, Wacki, Woo." Her broad navel is creased in a Howdy Doody grin.

Something derisive about that grin, the agent decides. He turns back to Khalidi.

"How old is your grandmother?" he asks quietly.

"Ninety-two."

"And she wants braces on her teeth?"

Youssef nods. "She believes straight teeth will help her find a man and perhaps marry again."

Ptolemy takes a deep breath and stands. "I am not going to pay for your lunch," he says firmly.

Khalidi looks as if he may weep. The agent lifts a hand in farewell.

"Good-bye," he says, and turns away.

"Long time no see," Youssef says.

Ptolemy turns back. "No," he says, "you've got that wrong. You only say that when—" He stops suddenly. "Yeah, Joe," he says with a feeble smile, "long time no see."

Manhattan, NY

A humongous cocktail party, paid for by Marilyn Taylor Merchandise, Inc., is held on the lower floors of the East 63rd Street town house. Guests and gate-crashers include customers, suppliers, reporters, photographers, authors, starlets, bankers, politicians, NYPD officers of high and low rank, television anchorpersons, attorneys, agents, talk-show hosts, stockbrokers, drama critics, models, actors, producers, directors, real-estate magnates, fashion designers, editors, publishers, two pimps, four hookers, and one congressman. The Mayor and Governor also stop by briefly to pay their respects.

There is a well-supplied bar on each of three floors, and on the second is an enormous buffet dominated by a huge ice sculpture of Marilyn, naked, in the pose of Diana as a huntress with bow and arrow.

The flesh and blood Marilyn is at her scintillating best. Clad in a gold lamé jumpsuit and carrying a flute of champagne, she moves blithely through the throng, bestowing air kisses on friends and strangers alike. Many guests comment on how ravishing she looks, with a special glow that makes more than one woman wonder if she might be pregnant.

The invitations specify "5 to 10 P.M.," but the hours pass, the buffet is replenished, the bars never run dry, and no one wants to go home. The hostess continues to circulate indefatigably, acting more like The Flying Nun than Attila the Huness.

She is still wired when, shortly before midnight, she clasps Lieutenant McBryde lightly by the arm. "Having a good time, toots?" she asks.

"Great party," he assures her. "But you should have banned smoking."

"Oh, sure," she says. "And screwing afterward. Get yourself another drink, and let's go upstairs." Then when she sees his expression: "Not for fun and games, dummy; I've got to talk to you."

They sit on the edge of her bed, the door closed.

"You sober?" she asks him.

"Of course I'm sober. I've only had three drinks."

"Five," she says. "I counted."

He laughs. "You don't miss much, do you? But I *am* sober."

"Good," she says, "because I want to talk a deal."

"What kind of a deal?" he asks cautiously.

"Our bicoastal marriage—it's on?"

"I explained to you—" he starts.

"I know what you explained, about having kids and all. But the marriage part is settled—correct?"

He nods.

"All right," she says. "Now about the kids . . . I talked to Doc Primster, and he says he may be able to reverse my tubal ligation. It'll mean tricky surgery, but I'm willing to go through with it."

McBryde puts an arm about her shoulders. "I love you even more for that, but I won't let you do it."

"As long as you know that I will if that's the way you want it."

"But I don't," he says earnestly. "That's no way to start a marriage, with you leaving the altar to have a date with a surgeon."

"There *is* another way," she says, looking at him directly. "Primster told me, but I should have thought of it myself."

"Oh? What is it?"

"Eric Bannon contributed his sperm. It'll be used to fertilize my eggs, and the four-cell embryos will be transferred to Eve's womb. And, with luck, one of the embryos will eventually be brought to term. A baby! You understand all that?"

"Sure."

"Well," Marilyn says, speaking slowly and carefully, "Primster says there is absolutely no reason why you and I can't do exactly the same thing. My eggs, your sperm. I'll get the embryos implanted in *me*. I'll be the real momma and you'll be the real poppa. It'll be our child, yours and mine. Get it?"

McBryde is outraged. "You mean," he says heatedly, "I've got to go into that stupid Masturbatorium and flog my bratwurst?"

The Most Beautiful Woman in the World smiles sweetly.

"I'll lend a hand," she says.